Fuzzy
and
The Boys

BY CARL A. OTTO

FOXTAIL FLASH KNUCKLES BUGS SQUAREHEAD

FUZZY

Copyright © 2006 by Carl A. Otto.

Printed in the United States. All rights reserved.

ISBN 1-58597-373-4

Library of Congress Control Number: 2005937467

LEATHERS
PUBLISHING

4500 College Boulevard
Overland Park, KS 66211
888-888-7696
www.leatherspublishing.com

This book is dedicated to Dr. Harvey Watson, my good friend, my advisor, my editor and my former colleague. His wise and timely advice, as well as his professional editing, was so essential in the completion of this work. As a published author and a veteran educator, Dr. Watson's keen knowledge of writing and of literature was exceedingly helpful to this old alley cat.

Author's Note

Fuzzy and the Boys is my first attempt at writing fiction. I started by writing a number of short fictional stories. Then I wrote one I called "The Sink Hole." It was a story about a group of curious 12-year-old kids. I had also written a number of other stories and had sent them to my friend, Harvey Watson, for his critique. He advised me to change the names of the characters in some of my other stories and incorporate the names of the kids I had used in "The Sink Hole. So I did. The stories seemed to fall together quite well. I am confident my work will be of interest to a wide range of readers, from kids to old geezers like myself.

I am a firm believer that a story does not need to contain descriptions of steamy sex in order to depict expressions of love and affection; however, in order to tell an accurate story about the habits of young kids, one needs to be frank and honest. In so doing, I feel the use of common slang and swear words are appropriate. I worked with kids for 40 years and found it was a rare kid indeed who would not lie in order to advance his/her agenda, or who was unaware of crude language. Language and/or an occasional fib are not the measure a good kid, a bad kid or a great kid.

There is no use of the Lord's name in vain or of vulgar language in this writing; however, if you are offended by the occasional use of crude words like shit, piss, fart, damn, hell, bastard and son of a bitch, you probably should not read this book. You might also be an individual who does not really know your own kids.

I have written and published two other books, both of which were collections of short true stories about my own life experiences. I called the first one *A Sauerkraut Sandwich, a Runny Nose and a Wet Sleeve;* the second was titled *A Sauerkraut Pancake, a Two-Wheeled Tricycle and Dancing the Cow Slurry Flop.* I have been a bit overwhelmed by the positive responses my writings have received.

I suppose the greatest satisfaction I have received from my writings has been in the many letters, e-mails and personal comments I have gotten from readers all across this country. I have a collection of letters from people from California to New York; from Texas to Minnesota; and from Florida to Alaska.

I would love to hear from you individuals who read this story. My home and e-mail addresses are both in the back of the book. I look forward to hearing from you soon!

Foreword

This is a series of stories about the antics of a tough little runaway girl from South Carolina, four young country boys from southeast Kansas and one innocent city boy from Topeka. Most of the action takes place in or around a small one-time coal mining settlement in southeast Kansas known as "Camp 4," which is within walking distance of the town of Owappaho. There are not many houses left in Camp 4, but one of the houses is inhabited by Owen and Elsie Tivitts, better known to the kids as Grandma and Grandpa.

These fictional stories take place during the late 1930s. If you are a teenager or a young adult as you read this book, you might think the characters are somewhat backward; however, if you are an adult of middle age or older, you might well identify with someone in these stories. But, then again, perhaps they are not too far from modern day reality either.

There are six main characters in the stories. Each story will feature at least one of the six, and may or may not include the others. However, most of the stories will mention all six of these energetic 12-year-olds. They are all good kids; however, they are not above stretching the truth, just a tad, in order to advance their agenda.

As the author wrote the stories, he did not intend to make it seem that any one of the characters was more interesting than the others. It was not until he was nearly finished and had scrutinized his own work, that he realized he had developed the character of Fuzzy, the little skinny, red-headed, freckle-faced tomboy of a girl, in the physical image of his late wife when she was a child, and in the spiritual image of the alley rat he himself was as a boy. At any rate, Fuzzy is in the spotlight much of the time. That is why he chose the title, *Fuzzy and the Boys*. All of the kids are past age 12 but not quite 13 during the summer of 1937.

Those pre-war days were times in which 12-year-old kids were not very worldly. They had not been exposed to the modern super-technical gadgets so commonplace today. The nearest thing to pornography to which they were exposed were the underwear sections of the Montgomery Ward or Sears and Roebuck catalogs. They were raised in the days when a man's word was his bond. They were raised in the days when you could actually buy something for a dime in the

Dime Store, and they were raised in a time when locking your house or your car doors was almost unheard of.

With few exceptions, the characters and locations are fictional; however, many of the stories are embellishments of events from the life of the author as he allowed his mind to wonder how it might have been.

Featured in most of the stories, and sprinkled throughout all of them, are problems all 12-year-old kids face, as the author attempts to interject into the everyday excitement of their energetic lives some lessons about maturation and sexuality, morality and integrity, curiosity and ingenuity, honesty and honor, love and affection, religion and even death and grief. The language is simple, but frank. There are some swear words, but none of them should be a revelation to anyone.

Table of Contents

Fuzzy Comes to Camp 4 1

The Sink Hole 15

Snipe Hunting 31

The Encounter with Bumblebees 35

Foxtail's First Kiss 43

Let's Try Smoking 53

What the Hell Is a Period? 61

Turnip Catches a Whopper 69

Vinnie the Hit Man 79

The Dead Giveaway 93

Let's Talk About God 101

Jake the Snake 107

Ketterman's Barn 121

Tater Diggin' 133

The Soapbox Derby 137

UFO 151

Fuzzy Has a Fight 159

Ernie's Special Request 165

The Long Shot 179

Tragedy Strikes Camp 4 183

Ernie Goes Home 189

Fuzzy Was Right 197

The Reunion of Fuzzy and Flash 201

Old Man Padget's Watermelon Patch 207

The Annual Camp 4 Picnic 217

Fuzzy Comes to Camp 4

THE MARCH NIGHT was cold and windy with a slight drizzle falling. Frank Thomas had been attending a County Commissioner meeting that lasted past 10 o'clock. He was hungry and tired and was looking forward getting home, fixing himself a sandwich and crawling onto a warm bed for a full night's sleep. He was driving along a county blacktop he had traveled more times than he could count during the 37 years he has lived in this present home. As he rolled along on this cold spring night, he watched his windshield wipers make those hypnotic passes back and forth, back and forth.

The road was asphalt from Middleton, the county seat, to Camp 4, where Frank's home was located.

He was fighting drowsiness by shaking his head back and forth every few minutes. He was also listening to his car radio. One of Frank's eccentric methods of fighting drowsiness while driving was to play his radio loudly and vigorously sing or hum along with the music. He guessed it was okay for a 67-year-old bachelor to act like a nut at times, especially when nobody was looking.

Frank was shaking the sleepiness from his brain as he rounded a curve. He thought, "Did I see a person standing by the side of the road back there?"

He slowed his car as he realized he had indeed seen a form of someone at the side of the road. He stopped in the middle of the road, opened his door and called, "Is there someone back there?"

A voice came out of the darkness, "Yes, could you give me a ride?" The voice sounded like that of a child.

Frank called, "Come on to the car; I'll give you a ride."

He waited with his door open as he could hear footsteps coming his way. A chill went over his body as he realized what a situation he was in; he had no idea who was approaching his vehicle. He had to fight the urge to slam the door and get the hell out of there, but somehow he felt he should wait.

When the stranger arrived at his door, it was obvious the person was indeed a child. "What in the world are you doing out here on a night like this? Go around to the other side. I'll let you in the car."

He reached across the seat and opened the passenger door. He then turned the heater up on high and set the fan motor speed on its top setting. The kid was about four feet five inches tall, slender in build and shaking like a leaf. In the dimness of the car, Frank could not tell whether his new passenger was a boy or a girl. At that point, the only consideration was getting this kid warm.

Frank asked, "Are you alone, or is there someone else back there needing help?"

Through chattering teeth, the kid answered, "I'm alone."

After he started the car moving, Frank asked, "What is your name?"

"Marvelle."

"How old are you."

"Sixteen." After a short pauses she added, "Ain't this night a bitch?"

Frank could not discern within 10 years how old this child was. He thought, "That voice is not a day over 12. But she sure must be a tough little fart."

Frank asked, "Where you from?"

She told him she was from South Carolina and had hitchhiked a ride with a truck driver all the way to Kansas. She told him the driver had treated her fine, at first, but that he had started getting weird. They had stopped at a truck stop in Middleton where she went to the restroom. She said she crawled out the restroom window and ran into the night. She had been walking and hiding since dark.

Frank assured the kid she was safe with him. He said, "Now, Marvelle, it is late and there is not much I can do this time of night; you are cold and wet and you need to get dried out before you catch a death of a cold. I'm going to take you on home with me now, but I promise you, I'll get you back home."

She interrupted him, saying, "No, no, I can't go back home. Please, mister, don't try to make me go back to South Carolina."

"Okay, okay. For now we will just go to my house where you can get warm and dry."

Frank pulled into his garage. "You stay here until I go open the door and turn on the light."

He hurried through the downpour, getting wet before he could get the door opened. He turned on the outside door light and motioned for the girl to come on in.

Once inside he could plainly see this child was not a 16-year-old. If she was, she certainly was underdeveloped.

Frank was thinking, "What the hell have I gotten myself into? Here I am, an old fart who has always lived alone. I don't know a damn thing about kids, and I know absolutely zilch about little girls. Now, I find myself in the middle of a rainstorm, late at night, with a soaking wet little girl who is shivering. I'm not sure if she is shivering because she is cold, or if she is scared spitless of me."

He again assured her she was safe with him. "We have to get you out of those wet clothes. I don't have any kid clothes, but I have a pair of coveralls you can wear while your clothes dry. He gave her the coveralls, and she went into the bathroom to put them on. In the meantime, Frank opened a can of chicken noodle soup and put on the coffee pot. The kid looked more like a circus clown than a little girl when she came from the bathroom, but she had stopped shivering.

"Are you hungry?"

"I'm starved to death. I had a toasted cheese sandwich for dinner, but that's all I've had all day."

Frank tossed her a towel to dry her hair. She was barefoot, so he tossed her a pair of thick cotton socks.

"Here, put these on those cold feet." He pointed toward the table, "Take one of those bowls there, and dip yourself some chicken noodle soup from that pan."

He ran her wet clothing through the washing machine wringer and then hung them on hangers above the stove where they could dry.

She went after that soup like it was the best meal she had ever eaten. As a matter of fact, she ate it all. Frank had to open a can of pork and beans for himself. As he was eating the beans and sipping a cup of coffee, she asked if she could have a cup of coffee.

"Do you drink coffee?"

"Yeah, and I really need a cup right now."

Frank poured the child a cup of coffee, and she sat down on the edge of the sofa while she started to drink it, but after a few sips she set the half-empty cup on the floor, as she lay down on the sofa. Within minutes, she was sound asleep. Frank got a quilt and a pillow. He spread the quilt over her tiny form. She was limp as a rag, and never made a sound as he lifted her head and placed a pillow under it.

Frank sat back in his rocker and wondered what he was going to do. This was certainly a new experience for him. He decided he had better call the sheriff and report a missing child, but, true to past experiences with rainstorms, his telephone was dead.

When he started home from that meeting, Frank was tired and sleepy; now he sat wide awake. He sat in his chair watching this little girl sleep. She has not moved a muscle since she flopped down on the sofa. Her breathing was soft and steady; she looked like she should not have a care in this world.

"My Lord, she looks like an angel. But what is the history of this child who pleads to not be sent back home. What the hell am I going to do? I have not a clue as to what to do or how to approach this situation. There must be some government agency for these problems. Surely the sheriff will know what to do."

Frank was awakened by a loud thunderclap. He was still sitting in his rocker where he had fallen asleep sometime in the wee hours of the morning. He looked at his watch; it was 9:45. He quickly regained the realization that he had a child sleeping on his sofa. She was still in the same position and was still breathing deeply and softly.

Frank thought, as he rose to his feet, "Good Lord, I haven't slept this late in years."

It was still raining and the wind was blowing. The house was warm and Frank was thinking to himself, "Oh, how nice it is to have all these modern conveniences. Two years ago I would be building a fire in the coal stove and going outside to the toilet. Now I have hot and cold running water, a bathroom in the house, electric lights and natural gas heat. Man, am I ever spoiled! But now I have to do something about this little girl."

He went to the bathroom and then to the kitchen where he started his electric coffee pot and put some bacon on to fry. While he was stirring around in the kitchen, he saw Marvelle head for the bathroom, with the legs of those coveralls dragging behind her feet.

In a few moments, she was standing in the kitchen door.

"Well, kiddo, you slept like a rock, didn't you?"

She shook her head yes.

He looked at her for a moment and then asked, "How old are you — really?"

She started crying. For sure Frank didn't know what to do then. He just stood dumbfounded for a moment. Then he said, "Don't cry, Marvelle. Everything is going to be fine. I don't know what I am going to do, but I guarantee you will be properly taken care of."

She blurted out, "I'm 11 years old, and I'm so scared, I don't know what the hell to do."

He walked over to her and placed a hand on her shoulder. She lunged forward and buried her head in his chest, saying, "If you didn't see me last night, I know I would have died out there."

Frank held her and patted her back for a minute. He thought, "You damned old fool, the tears are streaming down your face worse than the kid."

Finally he said, "Come on, you little fart, let's eat some breakfast."

"Okay."

"How does bacon and eggs sound?"

"Oh, that sounds great."

He told her to have a seat while he fixed breakfast. She wanted to know if she could help. He told her there was orange juice in the frig and told her where he kept the glasses.

"Where are my clothes?"

"They are hanging in the living room above the heating stove. They should be dry by now."

Marvelle said, "You have a nice house. And you sure got a nice bathroom. I noticed you even have hot running water."

"Would you like to take a bath before you put those clothes back on?"

"Oh, would I ever! I ain't had a bath for a week. But I suppose you already knew that. I probably smell like a billy goat."

Frank had to laugh. "No, honey, you don't smell bad at all, but you go ahead and take a nice long bath. The towels are in that corner cabinet behind the door."

"Can I use that big pink one?"

"You use which ever one you want." He chuckled as he realized she had already checked out the bathroom cabinet.

While they were eating their breakfast, Frank asked, "What is your last name?"

She replied, "Thomas."

"Thomas! For crying out loud, that's my last name, too."

"No shit, is your first name Frank?"

He was thinking, "Wait a minute. I don't recall telling this kid my name. How did she find out?"

She continued before he answered. "My grandma used to tell me that my grandpa had a cousin in Kansas. His name was Frank Thomas. Are you Frank Thomas?"

"Yes, Marvelle, I am Frank Thomas."

She jumped up from her chair and ran around to Frank's side of the table and threw her arms around his neck, saying, "I'll just be damned, it's a miracle. It's a miracle."

Frank was stunned. He did have a cousin named Homer D. Thomas. Homer had moved to Kentucky years ago, and Frank had completely lost track of him. But another cousin had told him Homer died at least 10 years ago.

"What is your grandfather's first name?"

"Homer."

He asked, "How is your grandpa doing these days?"

"I never knew my grandpa. He died when I was a baby. All I know about him is what Grandma told me."

"What about your grandma? Where is she?"

"That's why I ran away. I was living with Grandma until she died; then they put me in one of those orphan homes. It was really the shits. So I decided to go to Kansas and see if I could find you. I never dreamed I would find you so quick. Can I stay with you?"

Frank was thinking, "For crying out loud, what am I going to do with this kid who cusses as bad as I do, and she is apparently a relative."

"What about your parents? Where are they?"

"I don't have any parents."

"Everybody has parents, honey."

"Well, I don't. I never ever saw my dad, and I don't think he ever knew I was alive. My mother is a two-bit whore who left me with Grandma when I was three days old. We never heard from her again."

Frank thought, "My God, this poor kid; 11 years old and what a load to carry! She has to be a tough little rascal."

He sat her down next to himself and said, "Now, Marvelle, I told you I would see to it that you were cared for, and I meant it. But I must inform the authorities in South Carolina that you are okay and safe with me. If we can establish documented proof that you are my relative, you may stay with me."

"I understand. But if I get put back in that damned orphan home, I'll just run off again,"

"I'll do everything within my power to keep you here. Now go ahead and take your bath. We have to go to the county seat and talk to the sheriff."

Twenty minutes later Marvelle came out of the bathroom with her dry clothes on.

Frank almost held his breath when he saw her. She had washed and dried her hair. There was no doubt her hair was her crowning glory. It was dark red and shiny, and it hung in curls all around the sides of her face and halfway down her back. Her dark brown eyes were sparkling as she said, "Okay, I'm ready to go."

Frank just looked at her for a moment before he said, "Marvelle, you have the prettiest head of hair I have ever seen."

"It's a good thing. I'm such a skinny little runt, I'm glad I have something going for me."

"Believe me, you will not always be a skinny little runt."

"I used some of your shaving lotion as perfume. It sure smells good and I didn't want to stink up the sheriff's office.

It was nearly noon when they walked into the sheriff's office in Middleton.

"Hi, Frank, what brings you to see me?"

"Jack, I want you to meet my granddaughter, Marvelle Thomas."

The sheriff got a strange look on his face and said, "Your granddaughter? Why, Frank, you old geezer, you have been holding out on me."

The instant he said granddaughter, he thought, "Why did I tell him she was my granddaughter? Everybody around here is aware I'm an old bachelor who never married."

He added, "Well Jack, she is actually the granddaughter of my first cousin, Homer, but since he is no longer with us, I am filling in for him. But we do have some business to discuss." The sheriff motioned toward his office.

As soon as he knew the details of the situation, the sheriff called his deputy in, and they set the wheels in motion. He told Frank, "Even in this day of modern telephones and telegraph, it will be a little while before we can hear anything. Why don't you and your granddaughter go grab a bite to eat and then come back around 1:30 this afternoon?"

They left the sheriff's office and started toward Frank's car. As they went out the door, he felt a warm hand grasp his little finger.

She looked up, "Well, Grandpa, where we going to eat?"

Frank could not describe the feeling that swept over him. He had always been secretly envious of his friends who had children and grandchildren. One of his closest friends, Owen Tivitts, has a grandson he was always talking about. Frank had a couple of flings in his earlier years, but he never had a serious relationship until he was 40.

At that time in his life, he was engaged to be married to one of the new Owappaho high school teachers; however, when the wedding date approached, she got cold feet and called it off. Frank was embarrassed; he was hurt, and he never "put himself up for sale" again. But he didn't regret his life. He realized he had avoided many problems his married friends had faced. But when that warm little hand took hold of his old gnarled finger and those big brown eyes looked up as she called him Grandpa, he experienced a feeling he never knew existed. And it was good.

As they got into the car, she asked, "What am I going to do for clothes?"

"We will go to the clothing store after we eat and buy you some new ones."

"We can get them a lot cheaper in a second-hand clothing store."

He answered, "Well, honey babe, we might just do that, too."

She thought to herself, "He called me honey babe. I never heard that before."

"Let's go get something to eat now. There is a nice restaurant on the square where I eat quite often. We will go there."

"Whatever you say, Grandpa."

They went to the East Side Café. As they entered, one of the waitresses said, "Hi, Frank, who is this beautiful little lady you have with you?"

Before Frank could answer, Marvelle said, "I'm his new granddaughter."

The waitress said, "She is your granddaughter?"

Frank didn't even try to explain the situation. He answered, "You bet your boots she is my granddaughter. Ain't she a dandy?"

The waitress answered, "Yes, Frank, she is a dandy. Do you want a menu?"

"Yes, we want a menu, two glasses of water and two cups of coffee."

Frank was thinking as they ate, "Oh Lord, I hope I am not getting this child's hopes up, only to experience a fall when we go back to the sheriff's office. But surely the Homer Thomas that was her grandpa has to have been my cousin."

While leaving the Café, Marvelle said, "I wish I would have taken my suitcase with me when I sneaked away from that truck driver. Then you wouldn't have to buy me very much."

"Oh, God," Frank thought, "I forgot all about that truck driver." That guy picked this child up somewhere in South Carolina and transported her across at least four state lines before he got to Kansas.

"Do you remember the name of that truck driver, or anything about the truck he was driving?"

"Yeah, his name is Ray Bormann. He has it painted in big letters on both doors of his truck." She went ahead and described the truck in detail. She hesitated before adding, "But he was good to me most of the way. Oh, he asked me some dorky questions."

"What did he ask you?"

"It was mostly personal stuff."

"Marvelle, tell me exactly what he asked you."

"He asked me if I had any hair between my legs."

Frank almost growled, "That rotten son of a bitch."

"But he didn't do nothing. But he was drinking whisky, and I just thought he was getting ready to do something."

"Make no mistake about it, Marvelle, he would have molested you. You did the right thing in getting away from him."

They went directly back to the sheriff's office and told the sheriff about the truck driver. They were still in the sheriff's office when the dispatcher came in and said, "You're not going to believe this, Sheriff. Ray Bormann's rig is over at Mason's Garage. He broke down two nights ago. He is holed up in the HiWay Inn."

Before the dispatcher left the office, the telephone rang. The sheriff answered.

After a short pause, "You are saying that the officials in South Carolina say their records indicate the only living relative of Marvelle Thomas is a Frank Thomas, in an unknown address in southeast Kansas."

He hung up the phone. "It looks like you have inherited a granddaughter, Frank. It will be official as soon as we can finish the routine paper work."

Marvelle was listening wide-eyed, "What is he talking about, Grandpa?"

He took her hands in his and said, "It looks like you will be staying with me."

"How long will I stay with you?"

"Honey, you are now officially my granddaughter. My home is now your home. You are going to live with me from now on."

"You mean that's all there is to it? I really don't have to go back."

"Nope, you are stuck with me now."

She ran into Frank's arms and began to cry with joy. Frank's eyes welled up, too, as did the eyes of the sheriff and the dispatcher.

From the sheriff's office, they went to the clothing store where Frank always shopped. The manager summoned a lady clerk and told her to help Marvelle select a new wardrobe. While Frank and the manager were visiting, the lady clerk approached.

"Frank, she does not want dresses. She wants overalls and shirts.

Boys' stuff."

"Well, I tell you what. Go ahead and fix her up with two or three outfits like she wants. I'll bring her back again after we get settled in good. Make sure she has underwear, girls underwear, that is, and nightgowns or pajamas and a new pair of shoes and several pairs of socks and a jacket and a coat. That ought to be enough for now."

Leaving the clothing store with a large sack of new clothes, Marvelle said, "You know something, Grandpa, I ain't never had this much new stuff in my whole life; I sure do thank you a lot."

He answered, "I am celebrating getting a new granddaughter. You know, this is a whole new experience for me. You are the first little girl I have ever known."

"I want you to know that when we get to your place, I'll show you how I can work, 'cause I want to earn my keep."

He smiled and answered, "We will talk about those things later. In the meantime, I have to learn how to be a grandpa. And we need to get you back in school."

She sounded almost shocked when she said, "Oh, shit. I never thought about school. Grandpa, I don't have any books or other school stuff; hell, I don't even have a pencil."

"Were you going to school before you ran away?"

"Yes. I was in the sixth grade. Oh, hell, I have missed almost two weeks of school. Do think they might put me back in the fifth grade?"

Frank explained to her that she would be in a classroom with grades five, six, seven and eight. ""The teacher will determine what grade level you will fit in."

They rode along without talking, as Marvelle seemed to be deep in thought.
She broke the silence with, "Is this March?"

"Yes, this is March 23rd."

"Well, I'll just be damned, if that wouldn't just sugar your cookies."

Frank laughed. He had never heard that expression. "What do you mean, honey?"

"I am 12 years old, and I didn't even know it. My birthday is March 20."

"How about that! I was buying you birthday presents and didn't even know it. Now, you won't have to work off that clothing bill. The new clothes were a birthday present."

"I'll tell you one thing for sure; you know a hell of a lot more about how somebody should treat a kid than them damn people in that orphan home did."

They were almost home when Frank mentioned his spare bedroom and, that she would be sleeping there.

Marvelle said, "I always slept with my grandma. Ain't I going to sleep with you?"

Frank started to laugh, but then he realized she was serious. "Oh, no, honey. You will have your own room and your own bed."

"That's one thing I really missed after Grandma died. 'Cause I couldn't remember not sleeping with Grandma. You really do sleep better when you're not alone."

Frank was so moved he had to choke back a lump before he continued. "Marvelle, it was okay for you to sleep with your grandma, but it would not be proper for you to sleep with me."

"Yeah, I suppose you're right. Somebody might think you were like that truck driver."

"And we wouldn't want that, would we?"

After he had her settled in and they had eaten supper, Frank said,

"Come on, we are going to down the street a ways."

"Where we going?"

"Just a couple of blocks. I want to introduce you to Mr. and Mrs. Tivitts."

She was beginning to get a frightened look on her face, "Are you going to make me stay with them?"

He stopped, turned facing her and bent down to her eye level. "Oh, no, honey. You are now **my** granddaughter; you are going to live with **me.** These people we are going to visit are my best friends. I want to show off my new granddaughter. I know you will like these folks. Marvelle, I want you to get South Carolina completely out of your head. If you ever go back there again, it will be with me, on a vacation."

Owen Tivitts straightened up in his chair and looked out the window. Then he got up and went to where he could pull the curtain back.

"Hey, Elsie. Come look at this. Here comes Frank Thomas, walking toward our house, and he has a little girl with him."

Elsie came to the window. "I wonder who that child could be. My goodness, Owen, just look how the setting sun is shining through her hair. She looks like she is wearing a halo. My Lord, she looks like a little Angel."

The Sink Hole

Ernest OWEN TIVITTS and his mother and father were visiting Grandma and Grandpa Tivitts. Ernie's dad was on an extended business trip to Texas. Ernie was given the option of accompanying his parents on the trip or staying in Kansas with his grandparents; he chose staying with his grandparents. The date was June 2, 1937.

He met this guy who was really a cool dude. They were the same age; both of them had just finished sixth grade, but neither one of them was very excited about moving up to the seventh grade. Oh, school was okay; especially phys ed and science class, but English and spelling were just not Ernie's can of worms; and he soon found his new friend, Bugs, and he seemed to like each other right from the start.

The day his folks pulled into Grandpa and Grandma's yard, Bugs was there, visiting Grandpa. After Grandma got done giving all of them a hug, Grandpa said, "Come here, Ernie, I want you to meet my young friend who is about your age."

This boy came over to them and Grandpa said, "Bugs, this is my grandson, Ernie; Ernie, this is Bugs. Shake hands."

Bugs reached out and grabbed Ernie's hand and said, "You want to go crawdad hunting?"

Ernie answered, "Well, I've never been crawdad hunting, but I guess I'm willing to give it a try."

They started off down this little country road. Ernie said, "I never heard of anybody being named Bugs before, is that your real name?"

"No, my real name is Lawrence, but since I have always been fascinated with bugs, everybody started calling me that. I suppose your real name is Ernest."

"Yep."

"Where you from?"

Ernie answered, "Topeka, Kansas."

Bugs said, "Everybody here has a nickname, so I'm going to give you one. How about TopKan?"

"Sounds cool to me."

They didn't get too far down the road before Bugs stopped and said, "See that little pile of mud over there in the ditch?"

"Yes, what about it?"

"It covers a crawdad hole." He said, "Watch this."

He reached over to the grass and pulled off a long stem that had a fuzzy end on it.

"This is called foxtail grass."

He removed the pile of mud that was covering the crawdad hole, poked the fuzzy end of the grass down the hole real easy like, and started moving it slowly up and down. He started to slowly pull the grass stem out of the hole; when the end came up, there was a crawdad hanging onto the fuzzy grass end with his claw.

"Wow! How about that?" Ernie asked, "What do you do with them after you catch them?"

"You either use them for fish bait or you eat them. They're just little bitty lobsters."

Bugs told him there was another kid about a half mile down the road who was a lot better at catching crawdads than anybody. "In fact, he is so good at it, his nickname is Foxtail."

Ernie laughed and said, "Foxtail and Bugs — are there any more guys with funny nicknames?"

"Oh yeah, there is Squarehead and Knuckles and Fuzzy. Fuzzy is a girl, and she's the only girl our age around here, so we let her run with us since she is a real tomboy; she can run faster than any of us boys. They ain't no more kids our age, unless you count some of them that might come out here to Camp 4 from Owappaho once in awhile."

"Is this a town?"

Bugs told him, "It ain't nothing anymore except a bunch of old houses. The town of Owappaho is just right over there." He pointed north.

Ernie noticed what looked like a small mountain ahead of them, near the road. He asked what the large mound was. Bugs told him it was all that was left of the old coal mine. The mine was Number 4 mine; that's why they call this little town Number 4.

He went on to tell Ernie there used to be a big square hole in the ground over by that tailin pile; that's what that big pile of dirt and rocks is called. That square hole was the mine-shaft. The shaft used to have an elevator in it; that's what the miners went down in and up out of the mine on. The elevator was also used to bring the coal up to the surface.

"Not long after the mine closed down, they took a big bulldozer and filled the shaft full of dirt; they didn't want some kid falling in it."

The two boys were approaching another little house in the settlement. As they drew near, a little skinny, red-headed girl came out on the road.

She said, "Hi Bugs, who you got with you?"

Bugs said, "Hi, this is Ernie; he's from Topeka, Kansas, so I named him TopKan, and he is visiting Mr. Tivitts."

Turning to Ernie, Bugs said, "This is Fuzzy."

"These lunkheaded boys around here call me Fuzzy, 'cause I have curly hair, but my real name is Marvelle."

Ernie looked at her for a moment and said, "Maybe they should have called you Marvelous. Bugs tells me you can outrun all of them."

"That isn't saying much. These guys are slow as turtles."

While they were talking to Fuzzy, two more guys came running down the road toward them."

Fuzzy looked up and said, "Hey, look; here comes Knuckles and

Squarehead. I wonder why they're in such a hurry."

The two came puffing up, saying, "You guys are not going to believe what we found."

Bugs introduced Ernie to Squarehead and Knuckles. They both said hi.

Knuckles continued, "You know that grove of trees of trees over there behind old man Cooper's place? Well, we was just over there, and there is the strangest looking sink hole we ever seen."

Bugs asked, "What do you mean? What's different about it?"

"It didn't sink straight down like most of them do; this one is going down at an angle, and it looks like a person could walk right down into the old mine."

Ernie didn't understand what they were talking about. He said, "Wait a minute — what is a sink hole?"

Bugs explained how there were old mine tunnels all over under where they were standing, and that sometimes the ground would give away in a spot and fall down into the old mine, and that would leave a sink hole. Most of the sink holes are only two to 10 feet deep, and they go straight down."

Fuzzy said, "What the hell are we waiting on? Let's go see that strange one."

They all headed toward the grove of trees Knuckles and Squarehead were talking about. The grove was located in a place where no houses or other buildings were located. It was out in the middle of a pasture, and the trees were small and growing close together.

When they reached the sink hole, Bugs said, "Wow! Just look at that! You guys are right. That sink hole is different."

As the ground gave way, the topsoil that contained all the tree roots just tilted downward. The small trees leaned over at an angle and almost obliterated the opening in the ground. The small area looked similar to a hinged kettle lid that had been pushed down into the kettle, instead of being tipped upward.

About that time Ernie began to realize his parents were probably wondering where he was. So he told all of them, "Hey, guys, I better go back to Grandpa's house. My folks will start worrying about me."

They all decided to go home, but they agreed they should keep the new sink hole a secret.

Fuzzy suggested, "I know what we should do. Let's all meet tomorrow somewhere, and we'll go take a good look at that thing."

Bugs added, "Yeah, and let's all bring a flashlight so we can look down in it."

Ernie added, "We got a flashlight in the car that will send a beam of light into the dark a long ways. I'll bring it."

Fuzzy said, "Hey, guys, we better tell Foxtail about this; he's going to want in on it."

They agreed Foxtail should know. They would all meet at nine o'clock in the morning in front of Fuzzy's house.

When Ernie gat back to his grandparents' house, his mom said she was getting worried about him.

His dad asked, "Where have you been?"

He told them he had met some more kids and they were playing together. Before they could start asking any more questions, he continued, "Boy, these kids around here sure do have some funny names. Bugs introduced me to four kids about my age; one is named Fuzzy, one is named Squarehead, and the third one is named Knuckles, and I ain't met the fourth one yet, but his name is Foxtail."

Ernie's dad laughed and asked, "What did they call you?"

"Since I am from Topeka, Kansas, they are calling me, TopKan."

Everybody laughed.

That evening, Ernie asked his grandpa to tell him about the old coal mines that used to be around here. His grandpa explained how the miners would ride way down into the ground on an elevator-like thing called a cage. Then they would work back in the tunnels digging coal out of what he called a vein of coal, using picks and shovels. They loaded the coal onto little carts that were like little railroad cars, and pushed the cart on the little tracks back to the cage, where it would be taken up to the surface. Once on the surface, the coal would be taken up into what they called a tipple. From there, it went through a series of shaker screens that separated it into different-sized lumps of coal, and it was loaded onto train cars and sold.

He explained that the big pile of dirt and rocks was what they had to remove in order to make the shaft and make the tunnels big enough to move those little rail cars around the mine. He also told about how the miners used what was called a carbide lamp so they could see to work. Many times, miners had to work while lying on their sides. The vein of coal could be anywhere from 18 inches up to several feet thick. It was long hard work. In the old days, miners worked 12-hour shifts. Once down in the mine, they never returned to the surface until their shift was completed. He told Ernie about how the mines would have what they called an airshaft. There was a big fan at the top of the airshaft that forced fresh air down into the mine. The fresh air would circulate through the tunnels as best it could, and the stale air would be forced out the main shaft. The big fan was inside a building, so nobody would get hurt by the fan or fall down the shaft.

The mine companies were regulated by laws concerning fresh air and the territories underground where they could dig. They had to follow maps, so they would know the location of roads and buildings. They were not allowed to dig the coal out from under those places, and they were required to leave pillars of coal every so often to support the ceiling of the mine. Of course, many times the regulations were not followed. That is why there are cave-ins called sink holes in nearly all areas where underground mines were located, especially in areas where the coal was not very deep beneath the surface.

Today, the mining companies use huge machines called shovels, which they have brought into the coal-rich areas. They use them to remove the dirt and rocks that cover the coal. This kind of mining is called strip mining. They are thinking about passing laws that will require strip miners to push the topsoil aside before they dig down and remove the coal, and then level the strip pit dumps and replace the topsoil. There are still deep mines in parts of the world where the coal is too deep for strip mining. Grandpa said at one time he worked in Number 4 mine; then later he worked for a strip mining company driving a bulldozer.

Southeast Kansas now has many acres of strip pit dumps and long open waterways called strip pits; about all these pits are good for now is for fishing and swimming. There is one out east of here called the razor pit that is a favorite spot for skinny-dipping.

Ernie said, "Skinny-dipping; I know what that is. That's swimming without any bathing suit. Did you ever do that, Grandpa?"

"Did I ever? Why, Frank Thomas and I still sneak out there once in awhile and take a swim."

Grandma spoke up, "I suppose the next thing you're going to tell him is that old Aunt Bessie goes out there with you two old geezers."

Ernie's mom really cracked up at that, and then everybody laughed.

Now Ernie understood what a sink hole was. He didn't know whether to be afraid or to be looking forward to tomorrow, but he slept well. His grandma and Mom had a big breakfast waiting for him when he got up.

Ernie's dad asked, "Well, son, what are you going to do today?"

"I'm meeting the gang at Fuzzy's place at nine o'clock, and then we're going to play ball or something; whatever they have planned is fine with me."

His mom added, "I'm so happy you found some friends your own age to play with. Now you do realize your father and I will be in Texas quite a long time, but we will keep in touch."

His dad added, "You are sure you want to stay here? We could be gone most of the summer."

"I'm sure. I really like to live with Grandma and Grandpa, and besides, there really is a good bunch of kids here."

Ernie's grandma assured his mother, "Now, Alice. I know every one of these kids he will be playing with. They are energetic and rambunctious, but they are great kids. Oh, one of them has a 'slight' problem with the language, but she never uses the name of the Lord in vain."

"She?"

"Yes, she. But I guarantee you, this is an innocent child with a heart of gold."

"I don't know why I am anxious. I know you and Grandpa are actually much more capable of taking care of Ernie than I am."

"Well, I wouldn't say that. But I will tell you that you and Henry should make this business trip into a second honeymoon. Grandpa and I will look after Ernie, and we will enjoy every minute of it."

Ernie's parents were ready to leave the next morning by eight o'clock. As they were saying their final goodbyes, Ernie reached behind the car seat and retrieved the big flashlight he had put there last evening.

With his parents now on their way to Texas, Ernie felt a slight pang of loneliness as he realized he would not see them again for a long time, but he really did love his grandparents, and he was anxious to get involved with his new friends.

He turned to his grandparents and said, "I'm supposed to meet the gang at Fuzzy's house this morning, so I guess I'll be going."

"Wait a minute, Ernie." His Grandpa said, "What are you going to do with that big flashlight?"

"Oh, you mean this flashlight?"

"How many flashlights do you have? Yes, I mean that one."

Thinking quickly, he answered, "I want to shine it down one of those crawdad holes and see what it looks like down there."

"Okay, but don't lay it down someplace and lose it; that is a good flashlight."

"I won't, Grandpa. I'll see you guys later."

It was nearly eight-thirty when Ernie started for Fuzzy's place. When he arrived, Fuzzy was sitting on the porch with her head down on her knees. When he got over to her, he noticed she had been crying.

He asked, "What's the matter, Marvelle?"

She didn't realize Ernie was there until he spoke. She jumped a little and looked up. "You remembered my real name."

"Would you rather be called Fuzzy?"

"It don't matter." She went on to tell him that her grandma had died and that she missed her. She told him she really liked Grandpa Frank, but she couldn't help thinking sometimes about the grandma who had raised her from a baby. He felt sorry for her.

She wiped away her tears with the back of her hand and said, "Oh, hell, I don't know why I get upset once in awhile. Grandpa Frank is really good to me; it's just that I ain't got no mom or dad or even a grandma to tuck me in at night."

Ernie thought, "My gosh, here I am feeling so sorry for a girl I'm about to bawl; I don't even know how to talk to girls. Yesterday she just seemed more like one of the guys. Now, this morning she is acting more like a girl. Bugs says she is our age, but she shore ain't very big. I bet she don't weigh 70 pounds."

About that time, Bugs showed up with a different guy.

Ernie said, "You must be Foxtail, the famous crawdad hunter."

"Yeah, I'm Foxtail, and I guess you must be TopKan?"

"I guess I am."

Fuzzy piped up and said, "I think TopKan is a dorky nickname. I'm going to call you Flash, 'cause that is the biggest flashlight I have ever seen."

Ernie thought for a little bit and then said, "You know what, Marvelous? I like Flash better, too."

Bugs said, "Fuzzy, you're right, Flash is better than TopKan."

Bugs seemed to be the leader of this bunch, so from then on Ernie was Flash.

They looked up to see Squarehead and Knuckles coming, and they all headed in the direction of the pasture where the sink hole was located. As they were walking along, Flash heard the familiar pop, pop, pop, pop, pop in rapid succession of cracking knuckles.

Bugs said, "Now you know why we call him Knuckles."

Ernie answered, "I have heard knuckles popping, but you must be the champ at it."

He calmly replied, "I am."

Ernie thought about asking where they ever came up with a name like Squarehead, but he decided to just wait for that little bit of information.

As they were walking along, Squarehead said, "Guess what I done last night."

Bugs said, "What did'ya do?"

"I farted in the bathwater and washed my face in it."

Fuzzy hit him on the shoulder with her fist and said, "Oh, you dumb ass, I suppose you're going to tell us you bit the bubbles?"

Ernie thought, "This looks like it is going to be an interesting summer."

When the six of them reached the little grove of trees and the mysterious sink hole that was located on top of the hill, they all stopped and turned the beams of their flashlights down into the opening. They were speechless for a minute or two.

Bugs said, "Holy cow, would you look at that!"

The flashlight Flash brought held six D batteries, so the beam it put out was quite intense. They could see all the way to the bottom. You know how the side of the road looks when it has been cut through a hill? The parallel layers of rocks sometimes are pointed up at an angle? Well, that is the way this must have been. When the cave-in started, the break in the ground must have followed right up those parallel rock seams. Their lights revealed an opening in the earth that was about 16 feet wide and four feet high. The opening went down at an angle. The overhead, after you got past a foot or so of topsoil and clay, appeared to be solid rock.

Bugs said, "What do you think, guys? Reckon we ought to go down there?"

Ernie said, "Oh, gosh, I don't know about that."

Fuzzy just started down the slope. They all followed her. All of them except Fuzzy had to bend over to keep from hitting their heads on the ceiling of the sink hole. The footing was rough, but they could all move without falling.

They were nearly on the bottom when Squarehead said, "I have heard my dad say they was places where he helped dig out coal that wasn't mor'n 20 feet below the surface."

Bugs added, This spot must be one of the places."

The next thing they realized, they were standing on a nearly level surface, and they could all stand completely erect. Knuckles was the tallest, but he was only five feet seven. They shined the flashlights around and could see tunnels going in three different directions; two of them went down into the water, but the biggest one went around a bend toward what appeared to be another cave-in.

Fuzzy said, "Hey, you guys, I think I feel air moving."

She wet her finger by putting it in her mouth and held it up; they all followed suit. Sure enough, the stale air was moving.

Knuckles remarked, "There is only one way for air to be moving down here. There has to be a downdraft or an updraft out a different sink hole."

Bugs added, "Yeah, there has to be another sink hole or some dug shaft ain't been filled up."

Ernie asked, "Isn't the air down here supposed to be bad to breathe? My grandpa said something about something called black damp?"

Fuzzy said, "Holy shit, let's get the hell out of here. Black damp ain't got no oxygen in it! It'll kill you!"

She was scrambling up the slope as she talked. They all went after her like squirrels going up a tree. Safely out of the sink hole, they stopped to gather their wits.

Bugs said, "We were probably right in getting out of there, but anytime air is moving in a mine, there has to be fresh air coming in somewhere."

Fuzzy said, "I heard that miners used to always keep a canary in a cage down in the mine, because a canary breathes real fast and runs out of oxygen before a person does."

Knuckles added, "That's right. The miners did keep canaries or some other little bird with them. If the little bird passed out, the miners got out of there."

Ernie asked, "Do any of you know where the air shaft was located?"

Bugs answered, "Yeah, I know where it was. But I don't think it is there anymore, 'cause some people live where it was, and there is a building where it used to be."

Fuzzy said, "Let's go over there and see if the airshaft is covered up."

They decided they shouldn't all go at the same time, so Fuzzy and Bugs went to the place where the shaft had been located, while the rest of them waited at Squarehead's place. Squarehead was supposed to pull weeds out of their garden while his folks were gone, so Knuckles, Foxtail and Flash helped him pull weeds while they waited. They had the garden weeded out real good before Fuzzy and Bugs showed up.

Bugs announced, "Guess what? There is a building right where the airshaft was located. And guess more whats — the air shaft is still there."

Fuzzy added, "And not only that, there is a big 'lectric motor with a big squirrel-cage fan blowing fresh air down the shaft."

Ernie asked, "Why would anybody put a building with a fan in it on an airshaft of a mine that has not been working for decades?"

Foxtail said, "There ain't no reason."

Fuzzy asked, "Who lives in that place? Do any of you guys know them?"

Squarehead said, "I live the closest to them, but we don't know anybody that lives there. I think they all work at night somewhere, 'cause the only time we ever see them is about dark, and then again at daylight. I think they must sleep all day. One of them must drive a truck, 'cause a truck is parked there sometimes."

Bugs said, "I tell you what we're going to do. We're all going to be detectives. We can start checking that outfit out. My Aunt Mable works at the Owappaho post office that delivers our mail here, so I'm going to ask her who lives there."

Foxtail said, "I'll find out if they have any kids. I never have seen any around there."

Fuzzy added, "Everybody knows old Aunt Bessie is pretty nosey; I'll go pump her."

Flash remarked, "My grandpa is a pretty cool old dude. I'll see if he knows anything."

Bugs reminded all of them that they needed to keep the sink hole a secret until they knew what they were doing.

That night after supper, when Grandpa and Ernie were playing checkers, Ernie asked him to tell him about the other people who lived around here.

His grandpa said, "Well, Ernie, they are all pretty nice people. This is the kind of a community where you can leave your doors unlocked or leave your keys in the car, and you don't have to worry about it."

"Are they all your friends?"

"Most of them; my best friend here is the grandpa of that little girl you boys call Fuzzy."

"Do you know everybody who lives in Camp 4?"

"Well, there is a family that moved into the community a couple years ago that I have never gotten to know. They don't seem to bother anyone; they keep to themselves. The rumor is they work a night shift someplace."

"Grandpa, you told me about how the coal mines were where all the men around here worked. Where do they work now that the mines are closed?

He told Ernie about several factories located close enough for people to drive to work, but most of the people from Camp 4 work in the aluminum plant in Owappaho.

"Did they fill up all the holes they dug while getting the coal out?"

Grandpa laughed and said, "My, you are full of questions tonight. But the answer is no; all those open spaces where they dug the coal from are still there, but they don't bother anybody, unless there is a sink hole. Then the county comes in and fills up the hole. I have heard that mushroom farmers sometimes will use old abandoned mines to grow their crops because it is dark and damp down there, and the temperature is steady. But I have never heard of anyone doing that around here."

Ernie went to bed that night with his chest sticking out several inches; he had solved the mystery. He couldn't wait to tell the others about mushroom farming.

So the next day when they met at Crouch's park, Ernie announced, "I have solved the mystery."

Fuzzy said, "No shit! Tell us about it."

"Those people are mushroom farmers."

"That might be true, Flash, but Aunt Mable told me the people who live in that house get a letter in the mail about every two weeks from a chemical company. The letter looks like it contains a check."

Fuzzy said, "I remember Grandpa Frank telling me about some guys being arrested for storing chemical waste materials down in abandoned mines."

Flash said, "Holy Karukus, I remember Dad reading in the paper about those people getting arrested,"

Bugs said, "Gang, we have to inspect that mine again. I think the only light we'll need is that big one of Ernie's."

Ernie got his big flashlight again, and they headed toward the sink hole. As they scrambled down the incline, they all detected a very familiar and unmistakable odor. Someone was smoking a cigarette, and the odor was drifting out of the new sink hole.

Bugs said, "Give me the flashlight, and you guys all stay close behind me — and be quiet."

As soon as they reached the bottom, they made a formation like chicks following an old hen. They walked about 30 yards before they came to a bend in the tunnel. As they rounded the bend, they could see a tiny shaft of light coming from a small space between the roof of the tunnel and the top of a pile of rubble — and they heard the mumbling sound of voices.

Bugs turned the flashlight off and went, "Shh."

And, wow! Was it ever dark. Ernie was holding his breath, and he was squeezed up against Fuzzy's back. Then she turned around facing him and put her arms around his waist. He then put his arms around her shoulders and pulled her up tight. He could actually feel her heart beating against his belly, and she could feel his, too. They just stood motionless for a long moment. Fact is, they were all huddled up real close to each other.

The voices on the other side of the small opening at the top of the tunnel began to fade away, and the little shaft of light went out.

In that absolute black darkness that was so black Ernie could not see Fuzzy's hair that was rubbing and tickling his chin, he felt her head turn up with her face right up against his chin. Ernie turned his face down; their noses touched; then their lips touched, and for the first time in his life, he kissed a girl, and she kissed him back. For that short moment, Ernie didn't know whether he was down in an old mine or on the moon. Neither of them said a word. Suddenly Fuzzy reached up, pulled Ernie's face down and kissed him again. They never mentioned to the others what had happened, but it was burned into Ernie's memory so deeply he would never forget. And neither would Fuzzy.

They all just stood motionless and silent for a long time before Bugs turned the flashlight back on and said, "I think they're gone."

Foxtail remarked, "Well, I think we all know now what it must be like to be blind. I don't think anything could be as dark as it was when that light on the other side went out."

They decided to remove some of the rubble at the top of the pile so they could get through to the other side. While they were digging away at the rubble, the airflow suddenly increased dramatically.

Bugs said, "They have started that big fan."

Fuzzy said, "I can hear it running."

They all listened, and they all could hear it.

They continued moving rocks and dirt from the opening until they could crawl through into the other side. Bugs trained the light beam around the open space; it didn't take a genius to see what was going on. The room was full of 55-gallon barrels; each barrel was coated all over the outside with roofing tar. Bugs flashed the light beam toward another tunnel; it was completely full of those barrels. There was no way of knowing what was in the barrels. The smell of tar filled the air.

After checking several tunnels, they came upon another place that had several big flat trays with potting soil in them. Some of the trays had small pea-sized mushrooms growing in them.

Fuzzy said, "Well, I'll just be damned. Those guys are storing chemical waste down here, and they're using mushrooms for a cover-up in case they get caught."

Ernie said, "You know something, Fuzzy? You cuss better than any girl I have ever known."

She leaned close to Ernie and whispered, "How did I do in another department?"

He looked both ways to see if any of the other guys were close enough to hear.

"Don't worry, they didn't hear me."

Flash never said a word.

Bugs said, "Well, fellow detectives, we have solved the mystery. Now we need to inform the police."

Ernie said, "Why don't we tell my grandpa? He's a smart old dude; he'll know what to do."

So that is what they did; they told Grandpa Tivitts. He called Frank Thomas and a couple other guys, and the next day they went down in the sink hole and checked out the kids' story.

Before the day was over, the little settlement was swarming with police cars and newspaper reporters, a guy from the radio station and people from all over who were just curious. They wanted pictures of the six kids, and they wanted to talk to the kids. They pretty much let Bugs do all the talking, 'cause it didn't seem to bother him a bit. Ernie was so confused he hardly knew what was going on, but that night when he was listening to the news story on the radio, he couldn't help but remember that every time they were being asked questions or taking pictures, Fuzzy was standing right next to him. Sometimes she was even holding his hand. But he didn't care; he really liked Fuzzy a lot.

The news stories revealed there were five men who were bringing toxic chemical waste to Camp 4 from nine different states. Hundreds of barrels of waste were stored in the old mine. The men had constructed a device to enter and leave the mine through the old airshaft.

They also lowered the barrels down that same shaft, and they did all the work at night.

Had it not been for a new sink hole and the curiosity of six 12-year-old kids, that illegal operation might never have been uncovered. Ernie personally was not concerned about all the publicity they received; the only thing that mattered was the time he spent with his grandpa and grandma and the friends he made during that period of his life. The time he spent in Camp 4 had more influence on him than any other period of his life. Bugs, Foxtail, Squarehead, Knuckles and Fuzzy — especially Fuzzy — are names he will carry to his grave.

Snipe Hunting

GRANDPA AND ERNIE had just finished eating supper and were sitting on the front porch.

"Grandpa, Fuzzy ain't no relation to us, is she?"

"No, Ernie, she is no relation to us."

"Well, she has Grandpa Frank, how come she always calls you Grandpa?"

" 'Cause she is my unofficial adopted granddaughter and I am her unofficial adopted extra grandpa."

"How did that happen?"

"When she first came to Camp 4 with Frank Thomas, who is really only a cousin of her own grandpa, she spent a lot of time with your grandma and me. And one day she told me that her Grandpa Frank was a swell guy, but he was an old bachelor who really didn't know much about kids; that she wished she had a grandpa that knew more about kids."

So I said to her, "Do you know what? I don't have any granddaughters at all. What do you think about you and me adopting each other?"

"What did she say?"

"She said, 'Cool. Now I can have two grandpas — Grandpa Frank and you.' I gave her a big hug, and she kissed me on the cheek, I kissed her on the forehead, and she has had two grandpas ever since."

"Wow! That is cool."

While they were talking, they looked down the road to the south and saw Squarehead, Foxtail, Knuckles, Fuzzy and Bugs approaching.

Ernie said, "Wonder what they are up to. It'll be dark in 30 minutes."

Grandpa greeted them, "Hi, gang, what's going on? You all look like you have a plan of some sort."

Bugs answered, "Yeah, we do, Mr. Tivitts. We thought it would be a nice evening to go snipe hunting."

Ernie asked, "Snipe hunting, what is that?"

Grandpa answered, "Oh, Ernie, that is one of our favorite sports around here. Didn't I ever tell you about snipe hunting?"

"No, you never mentioned it."

Fuzzy added, "Well, Grandpa, I think it's about time Flash got introduced to snipe hunting, don't you?"

"You are absolutely right, Fuzzy. However, since he is not all that familiar with the hiding places of snipes, you guys should probably consider letting him hold the sack."

Squarehead spoke up, "How come I never get to hold the sack?"

"Oh, you did too get to hold the sack."

"I only got to hold it once."

Foxtail said, "Big deal! I only got to hold it once, too."

Then Grandpa spoke up, "I think every one of you has had a chance to hold the sack at least once. You guys are more familiar with snipe hiding places, so it is only logical that Flash hold the sack while the rest of you round up the snipes."

Bugs added, "That's right. So it's settled. Flash will hold the sack and the rest of us will round up the snipes."

"But I don't know anything about holding the sack. I never heard of snipe hunting before."

"That makes it even better. We will show you how to hold the sack."

About that time, Grandpa reached back under the porch swing and pulled out a big burlap gunnysack, saying, "Well, what do you know about this? Here is an ideal sack laying right here under my porch swing." They all laughed, but Flash didn't think finding a sack was all that funny.

Then Bugs had him stand astraddle of the sack while he stretched it out behind. Bugs then placed two small rocks in the sack opening and showed Flash how to hold the opening up so the hole was as big as possible. Everybody said, "Oh, that's great, Flash. You got it right the first time."

Grandpa stayed on the porch, but the rest of them all went across the road to a pasture that had quite a few small hedge trees and other brush in it. They went about two blocks out in the middle of the pasture where Bugs said, "Here is a good spot. We can place the sack right in the middle of the cow path. The grass is tall on both sides of the path, so the snipe can run right down the path and into the sack. Then as soon as they are in the sack, you close the opening. You got it?"

Flash was really getting excited. He was thinking, "Great! I get to hold the sack on my first snipe hunt."

As soon as it was dark and the sack was in position, Bugs told him, "Now remember, don't move, don't make any noise, just hold the sack open while we sneak around and chase the snipe down the path."

Ernie stood bent over and motionless as he held the top of that burlap sack open. He could hear sounds of his friends scurrying through the brush, as they seemed to be making a circle around him. Then he heard a fluttering sound that was similar to how a bunch of pigeons sound when they all take off at once. It startled him, but he never moved. His heart was beating so fast and hard he was afraid the snipe would hear it.

Then, after what seemed like hours, he could hear faint peeping or high-pitched chirping sounds as if something was hurrying down the cow path toward him. He continued to stand motionless and even hold his breath. Before he hardly knew what was going on, the sack he was holding began to move. He thought, "Hot dog! I have caught some snipes."

The next thing he knew, there was a flutter of wings all around him as some of these flying birds actually bounced off him. It frightened him so much he nearly dropped the sack, but he closed the sack and stood erect. He did not know what he had or how many he had, but something had run into the sack and Ernie had captured them.

He yelled, "Hey, guys! I got some, I got some."

There was no answer.

He yelled again, "I caught some snipes. I didn't get all of them, but I caught some."

No answer, still. He looked toward his grandpa's house where the porch light revealed people standing on the porch. He started toward the house with the sack of wriggling birds. The nearer he came the house, the more he could see that everybody who was on the hunt with him had already returned to Grandpa's house.

Flash crawled through the fence and started across the road. They all began to laugh like something real hilarious had happened. Even Grandpa was laughing so hard he was wiping tears from his face.

Bugs asked, "How many did you catch, Flash?"

Flash answered, "I don't know how many. I know I didn't get them all, 'cause a bunch of them flew and even run into me, but I got some of them."

Suddenly the laughter ceased.

"What do you mean, you caught some?"

He held the sack up. They could all see plainly that the sack contained something that was trying to escape.

Bugs said, "Let me see that sack."

Flash handed the sack to Bugs, and he felt the bodies in the sack.

"Well, everybody, I guess the joke is on us. Flash really did catch something."

"What are you talking about? The joke is on you."

Grandpa told Bugs to lay the sack on the ground and allow the birds Ernie had caught to escape. He placed it on the sidewalk in front of the steps. As soon as he released the top, three frightened bobwhite quail made their buzzing escape and disappeared into the darkness.

Then Grandpa told Ernie all about snipe hunting. He said, "I have participated in snipe hunts all my life, and you are the first sucker who has made suckers out of the pranksters."

The Encounter with Bumblebees

It was a lazy summer afternoon when Fuzzy and her boys were coming back from Owappaho, a town just a mile or so from Camp 4. They took a different route home from the one they took when they were going after a banana split at Hester's Soda Fountain. Fuzzy had suggested they go by the Owappaho City Dump.

Knuckles asked, "Fuzzy, why do you want to go by the city dump?"

"Because there is always something interesting there. You'd be surprised at what some folks throw away. One time I found an electric fan out there that was practically new; all there was wrong with it was the plug-in had one prong busted off. So Grandpa Frank just cut the busted end off and put a new plug on it, and now we have a good fan. And it's one of those oscillators, too."

Bugs added, "Yeah, but there is also a bunch of rats and flies and stinking rotten stuff out there, too."

"Of course, there is; after all, it is a dump."

Foxtail then said, "Fuzzy is right. One time my dad found a whole pile of good 2x4s and 2x6s out there; none of them was very long, but they was all good."

Flash added, "One time Grandpa told me he went out there to dump some stuff, and there was a perfectly good rocking chair. One arm was busted off of it, but he took it home and built a new arm. It's that varnished one that sets in the front room."

Squarehead added, "One time there was a little kid from Owappaho found a almost new tricycle in that dump. All there was wrong was one back wheel was missing. He put some different wheels on it, and it was good as new."

"See, guys. Like I say, there is always something interesting out there. Let's race the last quarter of a mile." Fuzzy took off running.

Squarehead added, "You guys go ahead if you want to, but you know none of us can beat Fuzzy in a race anyway."

By the time the guys reached the city dump, Fuzzy was right up in the middle of a pile of junk, and she was digging through it with a stick.

Squarehead went around on the north side where all the older stuff is pushed back in a pile by a bulldozer about two times a year. He wasn't there long before he came running out of there like he'd seen a ghost.

"Run everybody, there's a bumblebee nest back there in an old car seat. I could see them swarming."

"Ah, they won't hurt you," Fuzzy said. "Where is that old car seat?"

"Right around there on the north side. Clear over by the edge of the dump."

Fuzzy suggested, "Let's have some fun. We can all find a nice little flat board, like a lath or something, then we can stir up those bees and have batting practice."

Flash asked, "Ain't that a little dangerous? Sometimes a bee sting can really make a person sick."

Bugs added, "Is there anyone here who has never been stung by a bee?"

Everybody indicated they had been stung, so they all began to look for an ideal flat board to swat bees with.

Fuzzy said, "Show me where that nest is, Squarehead; I'll go stir them up."

"Right over there on the north side; you can't miss it. It's the only car seat over there."

Fuzzy headed for the north side, and the boys followed. When she got to the seat, she ran up to it, jumped on it with both feet and stomped up and down several times. Then she hightailed it away from the car seat. There was no doubt about there being bees in that seat; they came out in an angry swarm like a puff of black smoke and began buzzing in all directions around the seat.

The boys were back far enough that none of the bees were close to them, but they were after Fuzzy, and there were so many of them she didn't have time to do any swatting.

She began to yelp, "Oh shit, there's more of them suckers than I thought. Ouch! Oh, hell, another one got me. Damn it all, they're coming at me faster than I can run. Start swatting them, you turkeys."

Within less than 10 seconds, it was painfully obvious that Fuzzy and her boys had bitten off more than they could chew. They all began to yelp as bumblebees found their mark. Fuzzy got stung four times; Bugs got stung twice; Flash got stung three times; Squarehead got only one sting. Knuckles got one sting on the arm, and Foxtail escaped unscathed. Two of Fuzzy's stings were on her face, and within minutes her face was swelling.

They all headed for Camp 4. The Tivitts house was the nearest, so that's where they headed. They hadn't gone two blocks before Fuzzy's eyes were swollen shut, and Flash's left eye was closing rapidly. They were all worried about Fuzzy because she was by far the smallest of the group and she had the most stings.

Squarehead said, "Fuzzy, what was you thinking about when you just jumped up and down on that seat?"

"Yeah, Fuzzy," Bugs added, "you crazy little fart, if all those bees had stung you, it could have killed you."

"I think just four of them might have killed me. I'm getting sick, and I can't see — and I'm getting dizzy. I think I'm dying."

Flash said, "Oh, God, let's get her to Grandma as fast as we can."

Foxtail got on one side and Flash got on the other; they put her arms around their necks and each of them picked up one of her legs. They started running.

Bugs ran on ahead to tell Grandma they were coming. By the time the boys had Fuzzy in the house, Grandma was drawing a bathtub of cold water and had dumped two boxes of baking soda in the water.

"Bring her in here in the bathroom and put her in the tub, clothes and all. Flash was now carrying her by himself. He placed her in the water, and as she hit that cold water, she said, "What the hell is going on here?"

"You little fart, you have been stung four times. I guess the cold water is good for you."

"It is sure is cold. Where am I? I can't see."

Grandma spoke up, "You're right here with me, honey. Just relax. The cold water and soda is all I know to do. Are you still dizzy?"

"I'm a little sick to my stomach, but I ain't dizzy no more."

Grandma breathed a big sigh. "Oh, good. The worst is over." Then she added, "Did anyone else get stung?"

The three other boys all said they were going on home, and left.

Fuzzy looked up at Grandma through swollen slits for eyes. "Have you taken a good look at Flash? Them bumblebees got him, too."

She turned. "Ernie! My Lord, your eye is swollen shut. Where did you kids get into those bees?"

"Out at the Owappaho City Dump."

"Well, I'll just be switched, whose idea was it to go there?"

"It really don't make no difference, Grandma."

"It was my idea, Grandma. And I was the one that jumped up and down on their nest."

"Marvelle! You jumped up and down on a bumblebee nest?"

"There was a lot more there than I thought there would be."

"Do you think you have learned a lesson?"

"Yes, I have. But right now I'm about to freeze my tail off. How long do I have to stay in this cold water?"

"I think you have probably been in there long enough. Ernie, you get out of here so we can get this little 'bee keeper' out of those wet clothes. Go get a pair of your overalls and a shirt."

Grandma had Fuzzy stand up in the tub while the water drained out. She removed her wet clothes, and Grandma gave her a big bath towel. After she was dried off, Grandma said, "Now step out here and let me check you all over."

"My Lord, child, you have a big red spot on your back and one on your little peaked butt."

Fuzzy spoke up, "My little peaked butt? I ain't never heard it called that before."

Flash pecked on the bathroom door. "Here's the overalls and shirt."

Fuzzy put on the shirt, and it hung down to her knees. "I don't need them overalls, this shirt fits me like a saddle on a sow; it's got everything covered up."

"Is Frank home?"

"No, He went to a lodge meeting, won't be home until late."

"Are you feeling better?"

"Yes, but I would like to go lay down for awhile."

"That's probably a good idea."

She headed straight for Flash's room and crawled in between the sheets.

"Grandma, have you got a quilt? I'm still cold."

Grandma went after a quilt and then took it in and spread it over Fuzzy. Her eyes were still just slits and her entire face was swollen. Granny tucked her in and then bent down and kissed her on the forehead. "You rest, honey."

"You know something, Granny, that's the first time I can remember being tucked in like that."

Granny bent down and kissed her again.

As Grandma came out of the bedroom, Flash was standing by the door.

"Grandma, are you crying?"

"No, I just got something in my eye." She wiped her eyes with her apron.

Ernie said, "Grandma, I twisted the water out of Fuzzy's jeans and T-shirt and hung them out on the line to dry."

"What did you do with her underclothes?"

"I didn't see anything but jeans and a T-shirt."

Grandma shook her head as she went mumbling into the kitchen. "That poor child. I guess Frank does as best he can; he just does not know what to do."

As she entered the kitchen, Grandpa Tivitts came in the back door. He looked up at Flash and stopped in his tracks. "Ernie, what happened to your eye?"

"Oh, I got stung with a bumblebee. I also got stung on the back of my right arm and in the middle of my back. But Fuzzy got stung four times, twice in the face."

"She got stung four times! My God, that's worse than me getting stung 10 times."

"Now don't worry, Owen, she is well over the danger point now."

"Where is she?"

"She's in there in Ernie's bed, resting."

Grandpa went straight to the side of the bed and looked down at a sleeping Fuzzy. He came back in the kitchen. "My Lord, her face is swollen so tight it looks like she's going to pop off all her freckles."

"Grandma, how long will it take before this swelling goes down?"

"It'll probably be a couple of days."

"What's Fuzzy going to do? She can't see."

Grandpa said, "Oh, she will still be swollen in the morning, but I think she will be able to see by then."

"Grandpa, what if she would have got stung by more of those bees? There must have been a hundred of them buzzing around her. She could have got killed, couldn't she?"

"Yes, Ernie, that many bee stings can kill a person, especially a little person like Marvelle."

Flash wilted down into a chair. "That little turd. What am I ever going to do with her? She just ain't got no fear of anything. She just jumped on that old seat and stomped her foot, and those bees came swarming out of there like a storm cloud."

Then he turned back to his grandpa. "Grandpa, we have to go back to that dump and kill all those bumblebees."

"No, we are not, Ernie. Those bees serve a vital role. Mr. Gateway has a big field of red clover out there next to the Owappaho City Dump, and that clover would not make a crop if those bumblebees were not there."

"But they could have killed Fuzzy."

"Those bees will not bother you if you don't bother them. Come on out to the car with me; I want to show you something."

They went to the car, and Grandpa drove out to the city dump. He got out of the car and walked slowly right up to that old car seat. The bees were going in and out of the seat as he stood there. Then he slowly sat down on the seat. As he did, there was an increase in the number of bees flying around him, but none of them stung him. Then he slowly stood up and walked back to Ernie.

"When more bees came out as I sat down on the old car seat, I took a slow deep breath and held it. I was calm; I made no quick moves. I did nothing to frighten the bees, and, they left me alone."

"Wow! That was cool, Grandpa."

"I won't say calmness will always work, but very seldom does it not. So remember, the next time you are around bees, just remain calm. They will more than likely leave you alone."

"I have to tell Fuzzy about this."

Foxtail's First Kiss

ONE OF THE hardest things for a guy to do is admit he likes a girl. So here Foxtail is, 12 years old, and he finds himself starting to like Brenda Fortino, None of the guys ever thought they could actually like a girl; they have talked about girls lots of times and were pretty much in agreement that all girls were nothing but pains in the butt. Well, Foxtail shouldn't say **all** of them, 'cause Flash and Fuzzy sort of like each other. But Fuzzy is different than most girls.

One night after a boy scout meeting when Foxtail was hurrying home 'cause he didn't want to miss the last innings of a baseball game on radio, something happened that caused him to think different about girls, at least one girl in particular.

The meeting is always held on the first floor of the Masonic Lodge building. Most of the times Foxtail would hang around awhile and shoot the bull with Bugs, Squarehead, Flash and Knuckles before they all went home to Camp 4, but this time he took off running down the alley. There were no streetlights in the alley, so it was pretty dark, especially where the tree limbs hang out over the alley.

Foxtail was picking them up and setting them down pretty fast, when all of a sudden he ran smack into somebody. He really did not see who it was, but he knew it was another kid, 'cause when they hit, the other kid let out a grunt and they both fell headlong in the middle of the alley. As they started to fall, he could feel the kid was a lot littler than he was, and he didn't want to squash anybody when he fell on top of them, so he put his hands down to try to catch his fall.

As soon as he began to get his wind back, Foxtail said, "Oh, I'm sorry. I didn't know anybody was out here."

He could tell it was a girl he had run into when she answered, "It wasn't your fault. It is so dark nobody could see very good."

They both rolled over and sat up as Foxtail asked, "Are you hurt?"

"I don't think so. How about you?"

"Nah, I'm okay." But he did have a burning feeling in his right hand.

She asked, "Who are you?"

"I'm Merle."

"Merle Roberts?"

"No, Merle O'Brian, but everybody calls me Foxtail."

"Foxtail? How come they call you that?"

"Oh, it's 'cause I'm pretty good at catching crawdads with a foxtail grass stem. Who are you?"

"I'm Brenda Fortino. I just came out here to try to find my cat, and my flashlight quit working. It is so dark I couldn't find the gate that goes back in my yard."

"Yeah, there ain't no moon tonight, so it's really dark. I was cutting through the alley 'cause it's a short cut to my house."

Suddenly Foxtail realized his right hand was wet and sticky. He felt with his other hand and found he had cut the heel of his hand when he fell. It was obvious he had a pretty bad cut and was bleeding freely.

"Oh, my hand is bleeding. I better get on home."

"No, wait. My mom is a nurse. Come on in the house and let her see it."

She didn't wait for his answer. She took Foxtail's left hand and started pulling him toward her house. Their eyes had now become adjusted to the darkness enough that they could see the open gate that led into her yard.

They hurried to the house. Brenda opened the door and called to her mother, "Mom, there's a kid out here that needs your attention."

Her mother came from the other room, and as soon as she looked at the two of them, she said, "Good Lord! What happened?" She sputtered a bit more, "Brenda! Are you okay? My God, you are covered with blood!"

"I'm all right, Mom, but Merle cut his hand."

There was no doubt that someone had been cut. Foxtail had blood all over his front, and Brenda had blood on her arm and hand and on her blouse.

About that time her dad appeared in the room. "Oh, my God! What in the hell has happened here? Are you hurt, Brenda?"

Foxtail spoke up, "It's my fault. I was running down the alley and I didn't see Brenda. And my name is Merle, but everybody calls me Foxtail."

"Daddy, I was out in the alley looking for Fluffy. It was so dark he couldn't see me, so he ran into me, and we both fell down."

The first thing Mrs. Fortino did was look Brenda over to see if she too had any cuts. Then she said, "Brenda, go to the bathroom and wash that blood off and put on some clean clothes. Throw that bloody blouse in the lavatory and wet it with cold water.

Then she said to Foxtail, "Come over here to the sink and let me take a look at your hand. And by the way, Brenda, Fluffy is in the front room."

Foxtail's hand was beginning to hurt a lot, but he wouldn't let anybody think it was.

Brenda's mom asked him, "Are your folks home?"

"No, they went somewhere. They said it would be late before they got home."

"Is anyone at your house?"

"No. I stayed home 'cause I didn't want to miss the scout meeting."

"Who is your doctor?"

"Dr. McKee. Why?"

"Because you have a bad cut on your hand. It is going to require some sutures."

"Okay, but I don't want no stitches. And I don't want no shots."

"We'll let the doctor decide that. Now, son, I am going to call Dr. McKee and ask him to meet us at the emergency room. I am sure your parents would want you to see your family doctor."

"Are you guys going to take me to see Doc?"

"Yes, we are."

All the while they were talking, Brenda's mom was wrapping Foxtail's hand up tight so it wouldn't bleed anymore. He didn't know what to do, but Brenda's mom seemed to know exactly what they should do, so he just went along with whatever she said. She even had him remove his bloody shirt and put on a clean sweatshirt. Brenda put Foxtail's bloody shirt in the cold water with her stuff.

They went out to Fortinos' car, where Brenda and Foxtail got in the back and her folks got in the front. It only took about 30 minutes to get to the hospital in Pittsburg. Doc McKee was waiting at the door.

"What in the world have you been doing, Foxtail?"

"Oh, I had a little accident."

"Well, let's get in here and take a look at it."

Brenda asked, "Do you want me to stay with you, Merle?"

He didn't know how to answer her, but he really did want her to stay with him. But old Doc handled the matter. He said, "Why, Foxtail, of course, your wife may stay with you." Then he ruffled up Foxtail's hair and said, "I delivered this boy. Ah — let's see — has it been 19 years, Merle? And yes, honey, you may stay and watch the whole thing if you wish — that is, if your folks say it is okay."

Foxtail blushed and said, "Oh, Doc, you're a big old kidder."

It took longer for the shot that made his hand numb to work than it took to take the six stitches. Then Doc told him he needed a tetanus shot. He thanked Mr. and Mrs. Fortino for bringing Foxtail to the hospital, and they went to the car.

Brenda and Foxtail got in the back seat again, but this time she sat in the middle when they started for home.

Mr. Fortino remarked, "I heard Doc call you Foxtail. That's quite a nickname."

"They call me Foxtail because I guess I'm pretty good at catching crawdads with a foxtail grass stem."

"Oh, yeah, I remember when we used to do that when I was a kid."

The next thing he knew, Mr. Fortino was reaching back and shaking his leg, saying, "Hey, son, you'll have to tell us where you live."

As Foxtail awakened from a deep sleep, it took a few seconds before the reality of the situation hit him. Brenda was leaning her head on his shoulder, breathing deeply and sound asleep. She woke up when he started telling her dad where he lived. They couldn't have slept more than a 15 minutes, but they were both konked out.

When Foxtail told Mr. Fortino how to get to his house, he said he knew exactly where the place was located because he had a friend who lived there when he was growing up.

About a block from his house, Brenda reached up, took Foxtail's face in her hands and kissed him — right on the lips. "I'll call you tomorrow to see how your hand is doing."

Foxtail forgot he even had an injury. It was 10:45 p.m.

Mrs. Fortino was saying, "I had better go to the house with you and explain to your folks why you're late."

Foxtail's mom and dad were waiting at the door with very concerned looks on their faces. It's a good thing Mrs. Fortino gave him an old sweatshirt to wear. His mom would have fainted if she had seen that bloody shirt.

Foxtail said, "I'm going to bed. I am pooped." He reached the stairs before he realized he had not thanked Mrs. Fortino.

"Oh, I'm sorry, Mrs. Fortino. I didn't mean to forget to thank you, but I am sure glad you were there and really knowed what to do."

"I am happy I was able to help you. Good night, Merle."

He went upstairs to his room where he kicked off his shoes and just flopped down on the bed. If his hand was hurting, he didn't notice it. All he could think about was Brenda giving him that kiss.

He thought, "I don't even know her. I knew there was a girl living in that house. But she doesn't go to school where I go to school. I think one time Squarehead said the girl that lived in that house went to school in a different town where her mother worked."

Foxtail tried to go to sleep, but Brenda kept coming back to his mind. "She ain't nearly a big as me. Oh, God, what if she is like 10 years old." "She didn't have no boobs — or if she did, they ain't very big."

"But maybe she's older? Oh, God, what if she's 15? She is pretty strong, 'cause she really pulled hard on my hand when she wanted me to go see her mom."

Foxtail spoke right out loud, "You know something, dummy? You don't even know a thing about that girl. You don't know what color her eyes are, or what color her hair is."

Then the remark Doc McKee made came to mind: "Of course, your wife can come in."

"Is that the reason she kissed me? Oh, God, I wonder what she thought of that remark. That old fart. But he kids me about something every time he sees me. I have to get some sleep. I'm tired."

It was after nine the following morning before he woke up and went downstairs. His mom and dad were both home since it was Sunday. Merle had two hours before church started.

His dad asked, "How does your hand feel this morning?"

"Oh, my hand." He looked at the bandage. "Really, it doesn't hurt at all. But my shoulder is stiff and sore."

"Your hand must have slid over a piece of glass as you fell."

His mom spoke up, "Brenda called awhile ago, asking how you were."

"Do you know that girl, son?"

"Not really, Dad. I knew there was a girl living there, but I never run into her before last night — ha, ha, ha — I pulled a funny."

"You better call her, Merle."

"Oh, Mom, I don't want to call her."

"Now, Merle, that girl seemed to be really concerned about how you were. You call her."

"But what'll I say?"

He didn't want to tell his mom and dad she had kissed him.

"What did you say her name was, son?"

"Brenda."

"How about her last name?"

"Fortino."

"Oh, she is Italian? Hey, son, those Italians are hands-on people. I'll bet that little girl gave you a hug and a kiss before she let you out of the car last night."

You could have knocked Foxtail's eyeballs off with a toothpick.

He looked first at his dad, then at his mom, then back at his dad, then back at his mom. "Was I talking in my sleep?"

His dad said, "And how! You told us all about everything."

Foxtail turned and ran up to his room. He could hear his mom griping at his dad and his dad laughing. Before long, his mom was in his room and sitting on the side of the bed with him.

"Merle, your dad is just messing with your head. You were not talking in your sleep."

His dad appeared. "Son, I am sorry. I shouldn't be kidding you about anything like that."

"Well, the truth of the matter is, she did kiss me."

His mom brushed his hair back and said, "So what if she did kiss you? She felt sorry for you because your hand is hurt. There is nothing bad about that."

"Oh, I didn't say it was bad."

"Son, you are not going to believe this, but I was 12 years old the first time a girl kissed me. It was in front of my school locker after a ball game, and I couldn't go to sleep all night."

Then his mom added, "I was 13 the first time I kissed a boy. And do you know what? I still remember it as if it were yesterday."

His dad asked, "Who was he?"

"Donald Shipman."

"No kidding — Donald Shipman — how about that? Donald Shipman."

"Okay, big shot, who kissed you by the lockers after the ball game?"

"Hmm, oh, ah, I think we called her Corky."

His mom began to chuckle. "Corky Henderson, oh, boy. When Corky was 12, she told the rest of us girls she was going to kiss every boy in school before she was 13." Then after a pause his mom added, "And she had other plans before she graduated."

Foxtail asked, "What other plans?"

"Never mind, just go to the phone and call Brenda."

"I'll call her from the upstairs phone. And no listening in either."

"I promise I will not listen, and I assure you I will keep an eye on your dad."

"Don't worry, son, I have heckled you enough today. I won't eavesdrop."

He called the number his mom had given him, and Brenda answered on the first ring.

"Hi, Brenda, how you doing this morning?"

"I found out last night when Mom insisted she look me over real good, that I had a few bruises on my back, and my left elbow got skinned up a little, but nothing very bad. How is your hand this morning?"

"Oh, it's fine. Actually, I can hardly tell it is sore, but my shoulder is sore."

"That isn't too bad. Guess we could have gotten banged up a lot worse."

"Brenda, how old are you?"

"I'm 12, going on 13."

"So am I. When will you be 13?"

"Truthfully, I just turned 12 last month, but I will be 13 in 11 months."

Foxtail chuckled a little before he said, "Guess what? I was 12 two months ago. So I guess I'm just a month older than you."

"Did it make you mad when I kissed you good night?"

"Well, it surprised me, but it didn't make me mad."

"Was I the first girl that ever kissed you?"

"Well — yeah."

"Cool!"

"Yeah — cool."

"Do you like being a scout?"

"Yeah, I like it a lot. We do a lot of cool stuff."

"I have to go, Merle. I'm glad your hand is okay."

"Brenda. Have you told anybody about —?"

"No, I didn't tell anybody. But my dad saw me do it in the mirror."

"Oh, gosh, Brenda, was he mad at you?"

"No, he wasn't mad at all. But he did tell Mom. And then they both came into my room before they went to bed and told me about the first time they ever kissed anybody."

"Wow! My folks did that this morning."

"Did they really, Merle?"

"Yeah, how about that?"

"Do you care if I call you Merle instead of Foxtail?"

"Nah, I don't care. My mom still calls me Merle."

"I have a nickname, too."

"You do? What is it?"

"Turnip."

"Turnip! How did you get that one?"

"Oh, I helped my grandpa plant turnips one time, and they grew so good he started calling me that."

"Do you want me to call you Turnip?"

"I kinda like the way you say 'Turnip.' "

"I like the way you say 'Foxtail,' too."

"And guess what, Foxtail, when my dad told about this girl named Corky kissing him, Mom fell over on my bed and really started laughing."

The next day Foxtail could not keep from thinking about Brenda. He was a little confused about his own feelings, because he never considered girls to be anything but — just girls. Oh, he liked Fuzzy, but she was different. She could do anything any of the guys could do. Well, anything but go skinny-dipping with them.

He started wondering, "I don't think the other guys would mind if I asked Brenda to start running around with us, and I bet Fuzzy would like to have her join us. I think I'll call her and ask her."

So Foxtail called Brenda and invited her to join their group. Brenda was really pleased.

She said, "Oh, Foxtail, that is so sweet of you. I am sure glad you ran into me. We can see each other in the evenings or talk on the phone, but I can't run around during the daytime because I have to go to Middleton with my mom every day, except Sunday. And then I have to go to Mass."

"What do you do all day in Middleton?"

"I stay with my Aunt Josephene and play with my cousin, Angie."

"You got to school in Middleton, too, don't you?"

"Yes, Angie and I are the same age. We are also best friends. She is more like my sister than my cousin."

Foxtail hesitated a moment. "We can talk on the phone again. And maybe sometime you can miss a day with Angie and spend a day with us kids in Camp 4."

"I would like that. I'll talk to my mom and dad about it."

"Okay, Turnip, I'll talk to you later."

"Bye, Foxtail.

Let's Try Smoking

CAMP 4, AT one time, had a total of 16 houses with people living in every one of them, but with the closing of the deep coal mine, the population decreased dramatically. Many of the homeowners who were forced to go somewhere else tried to sell their homes, but in the real estate business there is an old saying, "There are only three things that determine the value of a piece of property: location, location and location. Consequently, some of the homeowners simply moved out and let the county decide what to do with their empty house.

Some of the houses were moved to Owappaho, one of them mysteriously burned to the ground, and three more of them are nothing more than meals for termites. One of the abandoned houses is located across the street from Frank Thomas' home; Fuzzy calls it her secret hideout. Frank and Owen are both active in their Lodge, so Fuzzy spends two evenings each month with Grandma Tivitts and Flash. Frank is also a district officer of some kind, so he is gone all day once in awhile. Whenever he is gone, Fuzzy will go into that old house, just to be alone with her thoughts.

Today was one of those days when Fuzzy had gone to her "personal hideout." This place is one she keeps to herself; she has not told any of the boys about it because that is where she goes when she is feeling sad or depressed about not having a mom or dad or no other relatives except Frank. He is really good to her, but he still has a lot to learn about kids.

The house is completely encircled with saplings; many of them are as tall as the eaves on the house. Between the saplings there are many gypsum weeds. Fuzzy had been in her hideout for nearly an hour when she decided to leave. As she emerged from her secret path, she looked toward the Tivitts' house and saw Flash coming out and headed in the direction of Owappaho.

Grandma Tivitts had asked Flash if he would mind walking to Owappaho and getting her a five-pound sack of sugar. It was only a one-and-a-half-mile walk, so Flash didn't mind. As he started to leave the house, he heard Fuzzy's sharp whistle.

She perked up when she saw Flash. "Hey, Flash, where you headed?"

"I'm going to the store in Owappaho to get Grandma some sugar; she is plum out. You want to go along?"

"Why not? I ain't got anything better to do."

So away they went, barefoot and carefree.

They passed a newly erected sign along the side of the road that had a picture of a handsome cowboy with a 10-gallon hat and a big smile. Clenched between his teeth was the puckering string on a sack of Bull Durham Smoking Tobacco. In one hand he was holding a cigarette paper with the tobacco held in it, obviously getting ready to roll himself a great smoke.

Fuzzy said, " You think you will look like that guy when you get growed up?"

"No, I'm going to be a lot better-looking than that guy."

"Oh, you think so? Maybe I ought to hang around and wait for you to grow up."

"You could do a lot worse."

"Flash, have you ever tried to smoke?"

"No. Have you?"

"One night my Grandpa Frank left his cigarette in an ash tray while he stepped out on the porch to pee, and I snuck a puff while he was gone. He seen me do it, and he landed on me like a sparrow on a horse turd."

"Did he give you a licking?"

"No, he just fussed at me and told me I was scrawny enough without doing something more to stump my growth. Then he told me he was sorry he fussed at me."

"Do you suppose cigarettes stunt a kid's growth?"

"Ah, hell no. If they did, I would be even scrawnier than I am. Grandpa Frank smokes in the house all the time, and I got my own stash of tobacco if I want it."

"Fuzzy, you have your own stash of tobacco?"

"Yeah. One day when grandpa was napping, I took one of his half-full sacks of Bull Durham and a little pack of rolling papers. I put them in my secret hideout, just in case I needed them.

"You have a secret hideout?'

"Oh, shit, there I slipped and said something about it. That's one place I have been keeping all to myself.

"Well, you have to tell me about it now."

"Okay, but you have to swear not to tell any of the other guys about it."

"Cross my heart and hope to die. Where is it?"

"Actually, you can't even see it for all the little trees and weeds, but there is an old run-down house in that empty lot across the road from our house."

"And that old house is your secret hideout?"

"Yeah, but now, Flash, please don't tell anybody about it."

"Don't worry, your secret is safe with me; you know that."

"Okay. Then when we get back from Owappaho, I'll show you my tobacco stash."

"Do you know how to roll a cigarette with one of those little cigarette papers?"

"Sure I do. You want me to teach you how?"

"I have always been a little curious about smoking, but I never really had a chance to try it."

"Well, hells bells, as soon as we get back, we'll go over to my stash and give it a try. I only tried it that one time when I sneaked a puff, but I've been wanting to try it. I just didn't want to try it all by myself."

When they reached the store, Flash went in and bought the five pounds of sugar, while Fuzzy stopped to pet a dog that was sleeping on the store porch. Then he told the clerk he wanted two Babe Ruth candy bars. While he was paying the clerk, Fuzzy came inside.

"Hi, Jim. How's Margie getting along?"

"Hello there, Marvelle. It's good to see you. Is this guy your old man?"

"Yeah, what do you think of him? He says someday he is going to look better than that Bull Durham guy. You think I ought to hold on to him?"

Flash was speechless. He just stood with his mouth open.

When they left the store, the clerk said, "I'll tell Margie I saw you."

"Tell her hi for me. See you later, Jim."

On the way out, Fuzzy stopped to pet the dog again; then she caught up with Flash.

"How did you get to know that guy, Fuzzy?"

"Oh, Grandpa Frank does a lot of buying stuff in that store. And one time the car broke down, and I spent a whole afternoon with Jim and Margie while the car was getting fixed. I got to know both of them pretty good that day. They're real nice."

"Here's your candy bar."

"Did Grandma tell you it was okay to buy that candy?"

"Yeah, she told me to get myself something."

"Thanks, Flash. I really like Babe Ruth bars."

An hour later Fuzzy and Flash were crawling in the back window of the abandoned house across the street from Fuzzy's home. Fuzzy crawled in first; then she turned and blocked the window.

"You have to pay a toll to get in."

"What do you mean — I have to pay a toll?"

"This is my personal hideout, and I charge a toll to anyone else who comes through the window."

"Okay, how much is the toll?"

Fuzzy never answered. She closed her eyes, pursed her lips and put her face in the middle of the window opening.

Flash grinned at her for a moment before he bent forward and kissed her.

"There, is that enough, Marvelous?"

"It'll do for now."

She went back into a closet, as Flash crawled through the window, and came back with a partial sack of Bull Durham smoking tobacco, some cigarette papers and a little tin box of matches. She also had six cigar-looking things she said were pieces of green catalpa beans she had cut into sections and allowed to dry.

She sat down on the floor and peeled off a thin sheet of that special paper, folded it lengthwise, opened the tobacco sack and shook some tobacco into the little V-shaped trough in the paper.

"This is the way you do it. You take this paper with the tobacco in it and roll this edge under. Then you roll it up into a little tube and lick the edge. That'll make it stick. See! Now you have a cigarette."

"Where did you learn to do that?"

"I watched my Grandpa Frank do it lots of times. Then I asked him if I could make one for him. He showed me how to do it. So, now ever once in awhile he will say, "Hey, squirt, roll me a cig."

Flash tried to roll one, but Fuzzy stopped him. "Shit, you're going to waste more than you use. See, there you spilled the whole damn thing. Let me do it for you?"

Fuzzy rolled two cigarettes, and they both lit up and started smoking. Flash tried to inhale, and it made him cough so much he about dropped his cigarette. Then they lit up sections of those catalpa beans. Fuzzy was coughing, too, but they both stuck with it until they were on their third cigarette and second catalpa bean cigar.

Flash began to look a little white around the edge of his lips, and Fuzzy started getting sick to her stomach. Between the two of them puffing and puffing, someone could have thought the house was on fire had the looked that way.

Fuzzy said, "I think we overdone it. I am getting sick; how about you?"

"I'm not getting, I am. Oh, gosh, Fuzzy, this smoking is sure not for me. I think I better go home."

"I'm going home, too."

Flash headed for home, but he was getting so sick he was about to throw up before he got home. He flopped down in the porch swing, but the motion of the swing had him on the floor within a short time.

All of a sudden he stood up and rushed out in the yard where he leaned on a tree and started vomiting.

Suddenly Grandma was at his side. "Well, you don't have to tell me what you have been doing. I can smell it. When I told you to buy yourself something, I did not mean tobacco."

"I'm sorry, Grandma, I never tried it before, and I swear I'll never try it again. I never had anything make me so sick so fast."

"I hope you've learned your lesson. Was Fuzzy with you?"

"Yes, she is sick, too."

"Is she at home by herself?"

"Oh, I think so."

"You go get her and bring her over here."

"I'm too sick to go get her."

"Oh, no, you're not. You are the one that bought that tobacco and got her sick."

Flash never told his grandma that it was Fuzzy's tobacco that made them sick, and he didn't mention buying the candy. He didn't want to get Fuzzy in trouble with Grandma.

"You're going to be sick for a while whether you are going to get her or leaning on that tree. You can stop and throw up on your way there and back. It'll be good for you. Now git."

He started to turn and head out for Fuzzy's house, but he didn't have to go; Fuzzy was coming into the yard.

Oh, Grandma, I'm sicker than a dog. Have you got anything that will cure cigarette-smoking syndrome?"

"Yes, honey, I do have something — advice — don't ever do it again."

"You mean there ain't nothing we can do?"

"The only thing you can do is drink plenty of water. That way when your belly starts the heaves, there will be something in there to throw up."

Flash added, "You mean there ain't a thing you can do for us?"

"Not a thing. It is just going to take some time."

"How long will it take?"

"You will probably be better by tomorrow morning."

They both groaned.

Fuzzy turned to Flash, "Oh God. I've heard of the 24-hour flu; now it looks like me and you have the 24-hour tobacco heaves."

What the Hell Is a Period?

GRANDPA AND GRANDMA Tivitts and Flash were sitting at the breakfast table when the telephone rang.

"I think that is probably Fuzzy. She said she would call me this morning."

Flash went to the other room and answered the phone. "Hello."

He turned and called back to the kitchen. "It is Fuzzy."

Flash turned back to the phone. "What are you going to do today?"

"I don't feel too good; I have a belly ache, so I don't feel like much action."

"Why don't you come on over? Maybe you and me and Grandpa and Grandma can play some Rook."

"Okay, I'll see you in a little bit. Bye."

Ernie went back to the kitchen. "Fuzzy said she ain't feeling very good today, so I told her to come on over and maybe we could play some Rook."

An hour later Flash, Fuzzy, Grandpa and Grandma were sitting at the kitchen table playing cards.
After a short while, Grandma looked across the table and asked, "Marvelle, are you okay? You look a little green around the gills."
"Oh, I'm okay, Grandma. I guess I must have eaten something last night that didn't agree with me. My belly is cramping."
As soon as that hand was finished, Fuzzy said, "I need to go to the bathroom."
After a short moment, Fuzzy called from the bathroom, "Grandma. Can you come in here?"
Granny arose and went to the bathroom. As she entered, Fuzzy said, "Grandma, look at this." She pointed to a bloody spot on her panties. "Something is bad wrong with me."
"Is this the first time you have ever noticed blood in your underclothes?"
"Yes."
"Well, honey, you have started your period."
A serious frightened look comes over Fuzzy's face.
"What the hell is **my** period?"
"Well, sweetheart, I guess nobody has told you about periods?"
"I know about periods; you put one at the end of every sentence."
"This is something totally different; it has to do with how a girl changes into a woman."
"I don't understand. Why am I bleeding? Am I dying?"
"No, honey, you are not dying. You have simply reached the age where your body is making a lot of changes. You are changing from a girl into a young woman."
"And I have to start bleeding through my twinkie to do that?"
Grandma chuckled at that remark.
"I should have known. I'm starting to get hair around my twinkie, and my boobs are starting to grow a little. What do I do about it, Granny?"
"First I want to emphasize there is nothing wrong with you. All girls have to go through the same experience."

"All girls? Does that mean boys don't have to do this period bit?"

"You're right. Boys do not have to 'do this period bit,' as you put it."

"Well, holy shit, that is a bummer."

"Let's watch our language, Marvelle."

"It ain't you that's bleeding through your twinkie."

"Well, not any more. I am past my childbearing days, so I don't have periods anymore."

"Childbearing days? Does this mean I can now have a baby?"

"Yes, this means you could now have a baby."

"Holy shit, I'm knocked up, and I ain't even had sex."

"No, you are not pregnant! But do you know about babies and how they are formed?"

"Oh, yeah, I know all about that stuff."

"You do? Well, tell me about it."

"I know that for a girl to get knocked up a guy has to stick his tool in the girl's twinkie and squirt in a bunch of little wiggly things. Then one of these little wiggly things gets together with an egg that is up in the girl. That's called fertilized. Then the baby starts to grow. It takes nine months."

"I guess that pretty well sums it up. Now let's take care of the immediate problem."

"What are we going to do?"

"I am pretty sure Flash's mother left some Kotex when they were here. I'll get them."

"Hmm. Kotex? I have seen boxes with that name on them at the drugstore."

"Let's remove your panties and your jeans. Now you're going to find out what those Kotex are for."

Grandma explained how Fuzzy should handle the situation and had her put on a warm robe.

"I will wash your panties, and your jeans if they are also soiled. While they are drying, I want you to go lie down in there on the bed and rest."

"What are you going to tell Flash?"

"I will tell him the truth. There is nothing wrong here. This is simply nature taking its course."

"Then I am okay? Should I tell Grandpa Frank about it?"

"Yes, you are okay. And I'll have Grandpa Tivitts tell him about it."

Granny leaned down to hug Fuzzy. "You are a strong, healthy girl. There is nothing to worry about. Here, you wrap this robe around yourself and go on in there and rest."

Fuzzy took the robe and did as Granny directed.

Grandpa called from the kitchen. "Hey, you two, what is taking you so long? Is everything all right?"

Grandma shook her head as she answered Grandpa. "Everything is fine. I'll tell you all about it later."

Grandpa got up from his chair and walked to the bathroom where he discovered Granny washing Fuzzy's soiled panties. As soon as he saw the red water in the lavatory, he understood the hold-up.

"She has started her periods, hasn't she?"

"Yes, she has. And, of course, Frank wouldn't know how to tell her what to expect. I guess times have not changes all that much since I was 12. Oh, Lord, I should have told her myself."

Grandpa went back to the kitchen table where Flash asked, "Is something wrong with Fuzzy? Where is she?"

"No, Ernie, Fuzzy is fine. Granny told her to go lie down and rest."

"But she said her belly was cramping."

"Yes, she did. Her belly was cramping because she has started menstruating."

"Menstruating, what is that?"

"It is more commonly called "having a period."

"Oh, I know what a period is."

"You do. What is it?"

"It is what women have to do every month. Dad told me about it."

"Just exactly what did he tell you about it?"

"He said that sometime in history some woman must have done something to really make God really mad, because women have to do this period bit every 28 days and men don't have to do it. And also, women have to carry a baby in their bellies for nine months before it is born. And also, women have to suffer when babies are born. That's when he told me I was never to hit or mistreat a girl. He said, 'Girls are entitled to everything a boy is entitled to, and one more. Girls are entitled to be protected.' "

"Your dad told you all that? Well, I am proud of him."

"Yeah, he told me those things, but I still don't understand what this period is."

"I guess it is about time you did understand. I have a copy of a physiology textbook in which there are several illustrations of the human reproductive organs. I will get it and explain this 'period bit' to you."

Grandpa brought the book to the kitchen table. Ernie looked at the book and remarked, "Gosh, Grandpa, this book was printed in 1922. Ain't it a bit outdated?"

"Yes, the book is outdated, but the illustrations in this book are as accurate as any book printed today. Our human bodies have not changed much in the past several hundred thousand years."

Grandpa opened the book to the page that showed a cross section of a female reproductive system.

"See this organ. It is called a uterus, and it is about the size of an average pear. And see these little tubes that lead up to these oval shaped things? These ovals are called ovaries. Each 28 days an egg is released from one of these ovaries. The egg then travels down this little tube and into the uterus. At this point in the cycle, the uterus is thick with, shall we say, building materials."

"You mean building materials that are needed to build a baby."

"Well, not exactly, but it is building materials necessary to get the egg started. It is at this time the egg is fertilized by a sperm cell. You do know where the sperm cell comes from?"

"I think so. It comes from the guy — right?"

"Right, it comes from the guy. If the egg gets fertilized, the girl is pregnant and a baby will be born nine months later. Now, if the little egg does not get fertilized, it passes on down through the uterus and out of the woman."

"Then what happens?"

"Now this 'building material' that contains a lot of blood cells is no longer useful, so it begins to break down. After about 14 days, it breaks down to the extent that is starts to trickle out of the woman.

That is when her period begins. That is what has just happened to Fuzzy."

"How long does the period last?"

"That varies with the women. Some periods last only a few days; others last a day or two longer."

"And a girl has to have one of these periods every 28 days for the rest of her life, right?"

"Right, that is, until she gets old enough to go through what is commonly known as 'the change.' "

"When does that happen?"

"Usually when a woman is past 40."

"As soon as the period is finished, the uterus begins to replace all the 'building block' cells. The walls of the uterus get thick again, another egg is released in the middle of the cycle, and the whole process is repeated. This process is called a menstrual cycle."

"Gosh, that really ain't very fair for girls, is it?"

"No. Nature is not fair sometimes. However, modern sanitary supplies make it a lot easier for girls than it once was."

"What do you mean?"

"I mean they can purchase sanitary absorbent napkins, called Kotex."

"Oh, Is that what is going on when a girl is 'riding the rag'?"

"Yes, Ernie, that is not a very delicate way of putting it, but that is what some crude guys call it."

"Does Fuzzy understand what has happened to her?"

"I don't think she does. Granny said it was a complete surprise to her."

"Well, I better go tell her."

"I think Granny is in there right now. She will tell her all about it."

An hour or so later, Grandma took a freshly washed and dried pair of jeans and a little pair of green panties to the bedroom to Fuzzy. In a few minutes Fuzzy came out of the bedroom and entered the kitchen where Grandpa and Flash were playing cards.

Fuzzy announced, "Well, Flash, you are now looking at an official woman. I'm having my first period."

Grandma grabbed her head with both hands, and Grandpa was

having a terrible time keeping from laughing.

Grandma said, "Marvelle, you do not announce things like that to the world."

"I ain't telling the world; I'm just telling Flash and Grandpa. They probably already knew it anyway."

"Are you going to tell Bugs, Foxtail, Knuckles and Squarehead?"

"Flash! She does not need to tell those other boys. This is a personal thing. It is nobody's business but hers. And don't you tell them either."

"Okay, Granny, I won't."

"I'm going to warm up a batch of soup I have in the frig. Is anyone hungry?"

Fuzzy said, "I could eat the north end out of a southbound skunk."

Grandpa just grabbed her and hugged her as he said, "Fuzzy, you little wart. You are one of the brightest spots I have ever had in my life. I love you like you were a blood granddaughter."

"I love you, too, Grandpa."

Turnip Catches a Whopper

THE GANG WAS gathered under the shelter house in Couch's Park, just shooting the breeze, when Fuzzy said, "You know what Grandpa Frank told me this morning?"

Bugs answered, "Well, we wasn't there so how could we know? What'd he tell you?"

"He said that the next three days would be real good fishing days."

"How could he tell, Fuzzy?"

"He said it was because the sign was right."

Knuckles said, "Maybe the sign pointed left." He laughed and slapped his thigh.

Fuzzy gave him a shove. "You think that is funny? Well, Grandpa Frank has a book called the *Farmers Almanac,* and it has a lot of stuff in it about signs."

Ernie added, "I hear Grandpa Tivitts talking about the sign."

Squarehead said, "We don't ever try to wean a calf until the sign is right. All I know is, if you wean a calf when the sign ain't right, that calf will bawl for a week."

Foxtail spoke up, "Great! Tomorrow will be a good day for going fishing, and not just because the sign is right."

"What else is right?"

"I'm going to call Turnip and see if she can go fishing with us."

Fuzzy asked, "Who in the hell is Turnip?"

"Turnip is Brenda Fortino. Don't you remember when I run into that girl out there at the edge of Owappaho and fell and cut my hand?"

Bugs said, "Yeah, we remember. How could we not remember? You didn't quit talking about her for a week."

Fuzzy said, "Oh, yeah, Brenda. You're going to ask her to come fishing with us?"

"Yeah. Most of the time she has to go to Middleton and stays with her cousin, but last night she told me she might be able to come to Camp 4 and spend a day with us."

Fuzzy said, "Great! I've been wanting to meet her. You go call her right now."

"I can't call her until evening, but I will, and then I'll call you guys."

Later that evening, Foxtail was on the phone waiting for Brenda to get on the other end.

He heard her say, "Who is it, Dad?"

Then he heard her father say, "I think it is that boy who ran into you that night."

She grabbed the phone. "Hi, Foxtail, what's going on?"

"I wanted to tell you we are going fishing tomorrow, and I was wondering if you could go with us."

She said, "Let me call you back."

Brenda turned from the phone and said, "Foxtail's family is going fishing tomorrow, and they have invited me to go along. Can I go, please?"

"Where are they going?"

"Foxtail didn't say that. But you met his folks, and they are nice people. Foxtail has all the fishing stuff it'll take."

Her mother said, "Okay, Brenda, but you promise you will be home by supper time."

"I promise. I'll be home by supper time; I might even have a great big fish."

Brenda called Foxtail. When he answered the phone, she said, "Mom said it would be fine for me to go fishing with your family."

He answered, "I didn't say we were going with my family."

Brenda came back, "The folks like for me to be involved in family stuff."

Foxtail caught on. "In other words, they wouldn't let you go if they thought you was with a bunch of kids."

"You got that right."

Foxtail hesitated a moment. "Can I talk to your mother?"

"Why do you want to talk to her?" she whispered.

"Because your mom and dad were awful good to me, and I don't want to do anything that would make them not trust me."

She whispered into the phone, "But I want to go so bad, and I'm afraid they won't let me go with just you kids."

"Let me talk to her."

Brenda turned to he mother, "Foxtail wants to talk to you."

Her mother picked up the receiver. "Yes, what do you want to tell me?"

"Mrs. Fortino, I think I must have said something that Brenda didn't understand."

"Oh, and what was that?"

"Well, she thinks it is going to be a family fishing trip, but it ain't."

"What is it then?"

Foxtail continued, "It is just us kids that hang out together every day. We ain't a bad bunch of kids. We don't do things that make our parents or anyone else get mad at us. Grandpa Frank said the sign is right for fishing tomorrow, so we decided to go. And I would like to have Brenda go with us."

"How many of you are there?"

"Well, there is me, and Bugs, and Knuckles, and Flash, and Squarehead and Fuzzy."

Mrs. Fortino asked, "How many of those strange names are girl's names?"

"Just Fuzzy. She is the only girl, but us guys all treat her real good."

Mrs. Fortino had a slight grin on her face as she continued. "Merle, I thought you were a good boy the night you ran into Brenda, but you have just proven it beyond doubt. I am very impressed with your honesty. And I am convinced that you more than likely would not hang out with a bunch of ruffians, so it will be fine. Brenda may go fishing with you and the rest of the kids tomorrow."

"Thanks, Mrs. Fortino. I'll come to your house tomorrow to get her."

"You are a gentleman. She will be waiting."

Mrs. Fortino put the phone back on its cradle, turned to Brenda and said, "Now little Miss Try To Deceive, we have something to talk about."

Brenda got a sheepish look. "Oh, what are we going to talk about?"

"In the first place, the only reason I am letting you go fishing tomorrow is because I trust that boy. I could tell from the tone of his voice that he was choosing his words with me so as to not get you in trouble."

"What do you mean, Mom?"

"Don't you act so innocent, Missy. You let on to me that you were being invited to a family fishing trip with his parents, and you knew his parents were not involved."

She started to pucker up, "I was afraid you wouldn't let me go."

"You are probably right. I wouldn't have let you go. I guess, in a way, I am glad you did fib to me. Otherwise, I would not have known what an honest boy that Merle is."

"He is a nice boy, Mom. And I like him a lot. I know I'm not old enough to date or anything like that, but I sure want to keep Merle for a friend."

She held her arms out. "Come here, honey."

Brenda went to her mom and they stood hugging each other.

"I'm sorry, Mom, I won't ever try to deceive you again."

"I don't think you will either, sweetheart."

"Thanks for letting me go."

The next morning Flash was up early as his grandpa and he were getting the long bamboo fishing poles down from above the car in the garage. Flash said, "Where did you get these long poles?"

"I found them at a hardware store in Middleton a couple of years ago. What gave you kids the notion to go fishing?

"Fuzzy said that Grandpa Frank told her the sign was right."

"Where you kids going to fish?"

"Out there at one of those clear strip pits south of town."

Grandpa thought for a moment before he said, "You know something? You have got my fishing fever up. I think I'm going to go, too, and I'm going to call Frank and see if he wants to go."

Flash clapped his hands together and said, "Great! We will have a good day. By the way, we are going to have another kid with us today, too."

"Oh, is that right? Who else will be there?"

"Brenda Fortino. Foxtail is going to go to Owappaho this morning and get her."

In the meantime, Grandpa Frank and Fuzzy were getting his fishing poles down from high up under the eaves of the garage.

He said, "Honey babe, what do you think the other kids would think if I went fishing with you?"

"Oh, Grandpa! I don't give a hoot what the rest of them would think. I would love to have you go." She grabbed him and hugged him."

With a great big smile, he answered, "I'll go, and I am going to call Owen an suggest he go along, too."

Frank went in the house where he reached for the phone receiver. He jumped as it rang a second or two before he touched it. He picked up the receiver. "Hello."

A voice on the other end said, "Hey, Frank, do you want to go fishing?"

Frank laughed. "Owen, you're not going to believe this, but I was just now reaching for the phone to ask you the same thing."

"Well, I'll be damned. That proves the old saying about great minds."

An hour later the whole gang was standing in front of the Tivitts house, waiting for Foxtail and Brenda to arrive. They were checking their gear. They had plenty of big fat worms. Grandpa Tivitts had some chicken liver. They had more than enough cane poles for everyone to have at least one.

Grandma Tivitts stepped out on the porch and said, "I'll fix a bunch of sandwiches and a couple of jugs of lemonade, if someone wants to come back and get them about dinner time."

They all liked that idea. Grandpa said, "That would be great. A couple of the boys will come get your fixin's about noon. We're only going to be about a mile from here."

Fuzzy looked toward Owappaho and said, "Here comes Foxtail and that little Dago girl."

Flash said, "Fuzzy, her name is Brenda, and her nickname is Turnip. Don't call her a Dago."

Fuzzy started to answer Flash, but he cut her off, "And she's not a Wop either."

She just reached up and tweaked Flash's nose.

After Turnip was formally introduced to everyone, the whole entourage started walking down the road toward the fishing hole. As soon as they arrived, Foxtail started helping Turnip get her hook baited and gave her instructions on how to toss her line in the water.

She did exactly as he had instructed. The line went out and the hook began to sink into the clear water; it did not get down three feet before something hit it.

Brenda was saying, "What'll I do? What'll I do?"

Foxtail said, "Pull the pole up. Looks like you got a good one."

The sign was right. Brenda was catching fish faster than Foxtail could take the fish off her hook and re bait it. They were putting the keepers in gunny sacks.

With nine fishermen strung out along the bank and everybody catching fish, they were beginning to wonder if the two burlap sacks they had would hold all of them. They were catching bass, bluegill, perch, crappie and catfish.

Grandpa Frank turned to Owen, "Have you ever seen fish bite like this?"

"Never in my life. I'm sure glad you kids decided to go fishing. I have had some pretty good fishing days, but nothing to compare with this."

Squarehead was fishing farther north than anyone else. He wasn't catching fish like the rest were, so he set out three poles, and he set the corks real deep. Everybody was laughing and talking and moving around on the bank of the pit; they were having a great time.

Suddenly they heard Squarehead call, "Hey, look everybody! There goes one of my poles."

They all looked out into the water where they could see a bamboo fishing pole being dragged through the water by a fish. Suddenly the big part of the pole stuck up out of the water about four feet, and then down it went out of sight.

Grandpa Frank said, "Sockaraputski, there is a big one on that line, and it's going to get away."

The end of the pole kept disappearing under the water, and then floating to the top again, only to disappear again when the big fish took a dive down deep.

Without saying a word to anyone, Turnip removed her shoes and dove headlong into the water. She swam toward the floating pole.

Grandpa said, "Good God, look at that kid swim!"

It didn't take her long to swim out to the floating pole and grasp it with one hand. Then she started swimming with one arm and her legs, as she pulled the pole to shore. Then while standing in water up to her waist, she bent that pole almost double as she pulled that big channel cat out of the water and tossed it on the bank. Foxtail immediately grabbed the fish with both hands in its gills.

Turnip climbed out of the water with a big grin on her face to the applause of the onlookers. Foxtail was beaming. He really liked Brenda, but now she was a genuine hero.

Fuzzy ran to her and hugged her. "That was the coolest thing I ever saw. Where did you learn to swim like that?'

"I have been swimming as long as I can remember. Most of the time, I swim with my cousin, Angie, in the Middleton swimming pool."

Grandpa Tivitts put his arm around Brenda. "This has been a great fishing trip. I'm so glad you could join us. But, now, I think we had better head for the house. You are all wet, and, besides, it's almost noon and Grandma has sandwiches and lemonade fixed. And we already have more fish than we need. We'll be cleaning fish until dark."

Fuzzy took Turnip to her house where she could put on some of her dry clothes while her own were drying out.

The two older men began cleaning fish as soon as they had eaten a couple of sandwiches. They put the big channel cat Brenda had caught in a tub of water; she wanted to take it home with her and show it to her folks.

Grandpa Frank said, "I know it is only a mile or so to your house, Brenda. But I am going to get my car to take you home when you get ready to go. We don't want that big fish to die before your parents get to see it, do we?"

She grinned. "Thanks, Grandpa Frank."

Grandma said, "Ernie, why don't you get your Monopoly game out. I'll bet you kids could get quite a game going."

Fuzzy said, "Great idea, Granny. I bet me and Turnip can just beat the tails off you turkeys."

So, while Frank and Owen cleaned fish, the kids had a Monopoly game.

It was 4:30 p.m. when Grandpa Frank stopped in front of the Fortino house to let Turnip and Foxtail out with a 10-pound channel catfish. As they started up the sidewalk toward the house, Mrs. Fortino opened the screen door.

"Look, Mom, look what I caught!"

"My Lord, you caught that fish, Brenda?"

Foxtail said, "Oh, you should have seen her, Mrs. Fortino. I was so proud of her I about busted wide open."

Mrs. Fortino was speechless. "Well — ah — what ... is it still alive?"

Brenda said, "Yes, it is. Foxtail said we need to put it in the bathtub, and put cold water in."

Mrs. Fortino was chuckling as she said, "My Lord, Brenda, I never saw a fish that big. Your father will faint when he sees that fish."

"Oh, Momma, I can't wait until he gets here." She continued, "Oh, yes, Foxtail said he could stay for supper."

"Oh, for heaven's sake, me and my manners. I got so flustered when I saw that fish, I forgot my manners. Of course, we want you to stay for supper, Merle."

Foxtail, Turnip and Mrs. Fortino were in the bathroom watching the big fish swim around in about 10 inches of cold water in the bathtub when Mr. Fortino came in the back door.

Brenda ran to him, "Oh, Daddy, you're not going to believe what I caught." She grabbed his hand and started dragging him toward the bathroom.

"What's going on here?" He looked in the bathtub. "For crying out loud! You caught that fish, Pumpkin?"

Foxtail answered, "She didn't just catch it; she dived into the strip pit, swam out to the middle, and drug it back to shore before she landed it. It was awesome!"

Her mother got a shocked look, "You dove into a strip pit after that fish? Oh, my God, Brenda!"

Foxtail added, "It was really cool. The fish was getting away. The pole kept going under, then coming up again. We were all standing there just sucking our thumbs, when Brenda took off her shoes and just dived in. Wow, can she ever swim!"

"Dad, I don't want to eat that fish. Do think old lady Snufflepuss would let us put it in her big goldfish pond?'

"She sure wouldn't if she heard you call her Snufflepuss."

"I can't say her name right."

Mrs. Fortino said, "Her name is Schneffelpaus."

Brenda turned to a grinning Foxtail, "See what I mean?"

He added, "We got one like that in Camp 4. Fuzzy calls her Skinnyflint."

Vinnie the Hit Man

ONE MORNING FUZZY and the boys experienced quite a revelation when the Streamliner passenger train began to roll to a stop near the Frisco depot. Everyone in Owappaho knew that train stopped only to let off passengers. Any time it did stop, all eyes were upon it to see who was coming to town. On this particular morning, the gang watched the train stop, the conductor hop down and place a little metal step at the bottom of the of the passenger car steps, and moved aside as a man in a black business suit, white shirt, black tie and black hat stepped down the stairs and off onto the railroad platform. The man was carrying a black case that was long and narrow. It was Vinnie.

His name was Vincenzo Bandoleni. Vinnie was a loner. He lived with his elderly mother in a small house in the eastern part of town, and as far as the gang knew, he was not employed. They never saw him in an automobile or even riding a bicycle; they never saw him talk to anyone, although me must have had some friends and acquaintances. Fuzzy and her friends assumed him to be an old man. He was probably in his late 40s or early 50s.

Vinnie's daily wardrobe consisted of bib overalls, dark blue shirts, old run-over work shoes, a denim jacket and an old beat-up hat. The kids never ever got close enough to him to know how clean he kept himself. He was never seen during the midday hours, only in those early morning days after a night baseball game. And he was sometimes seen shuffling along the street on his way home after a few drinks at the local beer joint.

Fuzzy retold how Elsie Jones and Mary Cenado told of walking home one night, and the girls were scared out of their wits by Vinnie. They said it was a particularly dark night, and they were walking along visiting when all at once they ran smack into Vinnie. As they bumped him, he put his arms around them; they screamed and he muttered something. The two began running like a wild animal was chasing them, and they never stopped until they were inside Mary's home.

Mary said, "He literally scared the pee out of me."

Fuzzy suggested the truth of the matter was, he probably was simply trying to keep them from falling.

Fuzzy and the boys were standing in front of Dino Lucciano's Garage and filling station watching as Vinnie crossed the tracks. They heard Dino remark, "Well, Its-a look-a like ole-a Vinnie he-sa been out-a on a hit-a some-a place-a."

Somebody said, "What'ya mean, Dino?"

"I mean-a, Vinnie has-a been on-a hit."

"You mean a hit, like a Mafia hit?"

"Yeah, Vinnie is-a hit-a man-a for da mafia."

"Oh, bull. How do you know that?"

Dino answered, "I don-a know-a for sure. All I know, is-a Vinnie some-a times-a jes-a disappear for a week or so. Den-a he come-a back wit-a he's-a little-a case-a and jes-a go about his-a business-a. I don't-a ask-a any questions-a."

The gang members stood with mouths open as they listened to Dino tell about the Italian Mafia. He told them, "Vinnie, he's-a probly go to Chicago. Dat's-a where he's-a get-a he's-a orders 'bout whose-a he's-a spose-a to whack."

As the kids were leaving Dino's, Squarehead said, "Hey, guys, Dino and Vinnie are both Dagos, so he ought to know what he's talking about."

Bugs added, "Ahh, I don't know about all that mafia crap. I don't think Vinnie is a hit man."

Flash said, "But, Bugs, we all seen him get off the train all dressed up like he'd been to a funeral or a wedding. We never seen Vinnie wear anything but overalls."

Foxtail then remarked, "I live the closest to Vinnie, and all I know is that he is a strange guy. Some days you never see him or his ma all day long. Then other days he will spend the whole day out there in that grapevine patch"

"What grapevine patch?"

Foxtail turned to Fuzzy. "Don't you know about his grapevine patch?"

"I don't know nothing about anything he does. Grandpa Frank told me to stay away from his place."

"Well, he's got four fences about a half a block long with grapevines growing on all four fences. The fences are close together, and Vinnie will be out there in that grape patch looking at the vines like he was hunting for something."

"What's he do with all them grapes?"

"Well, da, Fuzzy. He makes wine with them grapes."

Flash said, "Maybe he sells wine. Maybe that's his job. Lots of people like to drink wine. My dad drinks wine. But one time I sneaked a little swig out of his bottle and it tasted like vinegar to me."

Fuzzy added, "You're right about that, Flash. One time Grandpa Frank poured himself a glass of wine and then went outside for something. I sneaked over and took a little taste of it while he was gone. Yukk! It did taste like vinegar. I went and washed out my mouth right quick."

"You know what we need to do?" Bugs said. "Vinnie would make another real good detective project for us. We can investigate what's going on. Then we won't have to rely on what Dino says."

"Great idea. Let's go over to Crouch's Park right now and decide what to do."

So they all headed for the shelter house at Crouch's Park where they could sit down at a picnic table and make their plans. The first thing they did was elect a president of the investigating committee. Since Bugs was the best at talking to adults, they elected him. They didn't need a secretary or a treasurer 'cause they didn't need any money-raising projects and their investigation was going to be secret, so they didn't need no records kept.

So after the election Bugs said, "Okay, this is what we will do. We're going be very discreet about this investigation. Foxtail, you live pretty close to ole Vinnie, so you will be the main lookout. You keep an eye on what's going on at his place, and then call me as soon as you see anything suspicious."

"Okay. I can see his grapevines from my upstairs bedroom window."

"Good. When I hear from you, I'll call Knuckles. Knuckles, you call Flash, and Flash, you call Fuzzy 'cause you're always looking for a chance to call her anyway."

Fuzzy let loose a fist and whacked Bugs on the shoulder, and he let on like he was almost killed and everybody started laughing. Flash didn't know what to say because he really did like to talk to Fuzzy on the phone. She called him sometimes about bedtime and they talked about stuff. She was really pretty cool — for a girl.

Bugs continued. "Fuzzy, you call Squarehead, and then Squarehead, you can call me to let me know if everyone is on board."

Squarehead asked, "What do you mean by on 'board'? Are we going ride in a boat?"

"No, that's just an expression that means we all understand."

Bugs continued, "Okay, then it's all set. We'll just go about our business like we didn't have no investigation going on, but if any of us sees anything suspicious, we'll call a meeting."

That night, along about dark, Fuzzy called Flash on the phone. She said, "Hey, Flash, I have an excellent idea. Let's you and me sneak out to Vinnie's house tonight and do some snooping around."

"Oh, Fuzzy, I don't know about that. We have both been told to stay away from Vinnie."

"Nobody needs to know about it but you and me. We can say we're tired and want to go to bed early. We do that lots of times anyway, don't we?"

"Hey, Fuzzy, you don't have a very close rope on you, but I do. I could get in real trouble."

"Oh, pleeeezzee, Flash. Pleeeezzee, Just this once? I know we can get away with it."

Well, there was just something about how she said "pleeeezzee" that just kind of melted Flash's gizzard, so he said, "Okay, you come over and wait by my bedroom window."

Flash's grandparents were all engrossed in a radio program, so he told them he was tired and was going to bed early. They didn't seem to think anything about it. So he went in his room and put some clothes and an old quilt under the sheet so it looked like someone was sleeping in the bed. When he got done, he looked at his work and thought, "Hmmm, I did a pretty good job. That really looks like I'm under that sheet."

Then he turned out the light and waited for Fuzzy. It didn't take long because there she was, pecking on his window.

Flash grabbed his flashlight and crawled out the window. They went to the alley and then followed the alleys until they were out in east town. Flash about crapped his pants when they walked by Jerrell's bird dog pen and that dog charged the fence like he was going eat both of them.

Fuzzy just walked over to the fence and said, "Shut up, Jingo! Get back in your barrel!" And that dog did shut up and went back to his barrel.

"How did you know what that dog's name was?"

"I'm a dog person. I know most all the dogs in town — even the strays."

Their little town didn't have very many streetlights, and what there was were about as bright as a jar of lightning bugs. And if there wasn't a ball game or the Saturday night movie, nothing much was happening. They used to say, "All the sidewalks got rolled up and put away as soon as it was dark."

When they got out to Vinnie's house, Fuzzy sneaked right up to a window where there was a light inside and peeked in. She stood there for a few seconds and then came back to Flash, saying, "Vinnie is sitting in an easy chair with his head leaned back and his mouth so wide open you could stuff a baseball in it, and a big old cat laying in his lap."

"Is he sleeping?"

"Yeah, he is snoring so loud it's vibrating the curtains. And his old momma is sitting in a rocking chair knitting one of them Africans."

"You mean an afghan."

"Da. Yes I know what an afghan is. I was pulling your leg."

Fuzzy started toward the back of the house. Flash whispered, "Oh, Fuzzy, you're going get both of us killed. If old Vinnie is a hit man, he could rub us out and bury us in his grapevine patch. Nobody would ever know where we went."

But he followed her. She was whispering, "Let me see your flashlight."

"No, you can't have it. You would turn it on and Vinnie would see us."

"No, I won't. I want to find the handle on this cellar door. Never mind. I found the handle."

She slowly opened the cellar door and started down the steps. She whispered, "Come on down and shut the door."

Flash's heart was beating like a trip-hammer, and he could hardly breathe. It was so dark he could not see his hand before his face.

"Turn on the flashlight, Flash."

So he turned the switch, and it seemed like the sun had risen. The light was reflecting off some white boxes and off an entire wall of little box-like things that looked like post office boxes. Inside every box was the neck of a bottle sticking out.

Fuzzy remarked, "Wow! This is some stash. It looks like you're right about Vinnie, Flash, he must be a wine salesman."

"Fuzzy, we better get out of here — right now."

"Okay, let's go. We can talk about what we found later."

As they turned to start back up the steps, the flashlight beam revealed a long black suitcase-like box. It was the same one Vinnie was carrying the day he got off the train. Flash opened the case to look inside. The case was empty, but there were six molded depressions along its length. Each depression was obviously made for a wine bottle.

Flash turned off the flashlight, and they quietly slipped out of the cellar and hurried away from Vinnie's house. Neither of them said a word until they were a full two blocks nearer main street.

"Fuzzy, Vinnie is no hit man."

"No, he sure is not. I saw that case you were looking in. That is the one he was carrying the day he got off the train."

"Yeah. He didn't have a rifle; he had an empty case. I bet he was taking wine samples somewhere to sell them."

"That sounds logical, but maybe he had a rifle underneath the wine bottles. That would make a good cover-up device."

"Oh, boy, Flash, I thought we had the mystery solved. But now we have to find out what else might be in that long case."

"Oh, I wish I would have taken a better look while we were there."

"Let's go back, Flash. I bet Vinnie is still sleeping like a rock."

"No, listen, Fuzzy, I about had a heart attack the first time. I don't know if I could go back again."

"Well then, give me your flashlight. I'm going back to get a better look at that case thing." She grabbed the flashlight from his hand and started back toward Vinnie's house.

Flash just grabbed both sides of his head, looked up at the sky and said, "Grrr … I hear my dad say you'll never understand a woman; now I know why."

Then he called, "Well, wait for me."

When they arrived back at Vinnie's house, Fuzzy peeked in the window again. She whispered, "He is still sleeping just like he was awhile ago, and his ma is still knitting."

They quietly went back to the cellar door, opened it slowly and went down the stairs. Flash turned on his flashlight as Fuzzy opened that black case again. She pulled the lining loose and looked under the bottle molds. There was nothing in the case.

She whispered, "I guess this proves Vinnie ain't a hit man."

"This don't prove anything except that me and you are nuts. Vinnie could hide a pistol in lots of places, same as cops do. Let's get out of here. We can report to Bugs in the morning."

Flash turned off his flashlight, and they headed back up the stairs. When they opened the door to leave, there stood Vinnie with a double-barreled shotgun pointed right at them. They both froze in their tracks, and Flash nearly fainted. Looking up from down in that cellar, Vinnie looked like he was 10 feet tall and six feet wide. He was holding a flashlight that looked like a car headlight.

"Well, well, what do we have here? Looks like I have caught a couple of thieves. What do you think I should do with you two?"

Fuzzy cleared her throat and said, "You sure do have a nice wine cellar here, Vinnie."

Flash couldn't say a word. All he could see was that shotgun pointed at them.

"Are you gonna shoot us, Vinnie?" Fuzzy asked.

"Oh, no! Why would I shoot such 'special' guests? You kids are going to come in the house and meet my mother." He motioned with the shotgun toward the back door.

They came up out of the cellar, Vinnie closed the cellar door and they went into the house.

"Hey, Momma, come here. We have some late evening guests I want you to meet."

From the other room they heard, "What-a you talk about-a, Vinnie? We never-a have any-a guests dissa time o da nite-a."

"Oh, but, momma, we have very special guests this time."

"So, whats-a so special 'bout des-a guest."

"They are wine cellar inspectors, Momma."

"You mean-a da kind of-a inspector whats-a make-a good fertilizer?"

When she said fertilizer, Fuzzy looked at Flash and he looked at her. She ran over to him, and he hugged her, saying, "Vinnie, we didn't steal anything and we didn't mean any harm, we was just … we was … we was just … ah … we was here on a bet."

"On a bet, you say. Just what kind of a bet are you talking about?"

"I bet some guys that you were a wine salesman," Fuzzy broke in, adding, "and some of the other guys thought you are a Mafia hit man."

Vinnie's mother entered the room. She stopped in her tracks when she saw Fuzzy and Flash.

"See ammo vecci troppo presto, eh vecchi troppo tarde intelligenti. Vinnie! Deze is-a not dog or a cat-a fertilizer! Deze is-a kids-a. You no gonna shoot-a da kids-a?"

"No, Momma, I am not going to shoot the kids. I am just going to give them a lesson they will never forget."

He placed his shotgun in a rack above the kitchen door and told the kids to be seated at the kitchen table. Flash was surprised that Vinnie did not speak with an accent like his mother. As a matter of fact, his speech was more like that of a teacher.

"Now, what is your name, miss?"

"Marvelle Thomas, but everybody calls me Fuzzy."

"And how old are you, Marvelle?"

"Twelve."

He pointed at Flash and asked, "And your name, son."

"Ernest Tivitts. I am also 12 years old."

"All right, kids, you say you are proving some kind of bet you have made with some other kids. I believe you. It is too late tonight to do anything, but I would like to help all of you settle your bet tomorrow. So this is what I want you to do. You assemble all your other friends who are involved in this little 'bet' and have them here at my house tomorrow afternoon promptly at 2 p.m., and I will not call your parents, or the law, to inform them you were in my cellar without my permission."

Fuzzy spoke up, "We can sure do that."

"Good. And you are not to tell anyone about this plan until I say it is all right. Now, tell Momma goodnight, and I'll see you tomorrow."

The kids both sputtered a few good nights and headed home.

Flash was still breathing like he had run a two-mile race, and his heart was about to pound through his rib cage when he took a deep breath and said, "Wow! I thought we were goners when I looked into the barrel of that shotgun."

Fuzzy held her hands out to her sides with the palms up and said, "Ah, Flash, you ain't got no faith in the human race."

"I ain't got no faith! You little rat! Who was it that came running to me when his momma said something about making kids into fertilizer?"

"Okay, so I was scared, too."

"Now we have to get back in our own houses without getting caught."

They hurried on to Flash's house, and he crawled through the window to his room. Then he turned around and stuck his head back out to say something to Fuzzy. As he started to speak, she grabbed him by the ears with her hands, pulled his face down to hers and kissed him — right on the lips.

"Good night, Flash, I'll see you tomorrow morning." She turned and headed for her house.

By the time he got undressed and into bed, he realized he was so tired he could hardly lift his arms. As he drifted off to sleep, he was thinking, " I really like Fuzzy and I don't mind her kissing me like that, but I hope she don't tell the other guys about it. Surely she won't tell the other guys. I wonder if she kisses all the guys. I don't think she does."

The next morning they made all the necessary calls to assemble the "investigating committee" at Crouch's Park. At first, they had a hard time convincing Bugs and the rest of the gang what they had done. They had to convince them to agree to meet again at 1:30 so they could all go together to Vinnie's house. It took some pleading, but the others finally agreed.

So, promptly at 2 p.m. Fuzzy and Flash were introducing Bugs,

Squarehead, Foxtail and Knuckles to Vinnie and his mom. When they went in the house, they discovered Vinnie's mom had a big pitcher of lemonade and a platter of cookies on the table. Vinnie told all of them to have a seat while his mom poured each of them a big glass of lemonade.

They were all looking back and forth at each other wondering what would be next. Flash was so nervous he had to use both hands to pick up his glass. Then Vinnie started talking.

He stood while he talked. "Now my nosy little friends, I will tell you something about 'Old Vinnie' because I can understand why a bunch of 12-year-old kids would think there is some great mystery about me.

"Truthfully, I am a person who is what you would call a loner. I am a loner because I am still adjusting to a great personal loss. You see, before I came to live in this little town with my mother, I lived in Chicago and worked for a very wealthy family as a gardener, chauffeur and tutor to his children. I also had a wife and two teen-aged boys. I was living a very happy life. Then one day I received news that my father had passed away. I hurriedly assembled the things we needed for a trip, and we started to come here.

"We loaded our things into the car, and my wife and the boys had gotten in the car when suddenly a pickup driven by a drunk who was trying to get away from the police came directly across the sidewalk and our yard, striking my car on the passenger side. They said he was traveling over 100 miles per hour. My family was killed instantly before my eyes while I was locking the front door of the house.

"While my father was living, he made his own special blend of wine. One Christmas, I gave my boss a bottle of Poppa's wine. From that time on, my boss would serve no other wine to his guests. So when Poppa passed away and I lost my family, I moved back here with Momma and have continued to make the wine like Poppa did. I usually make two or three trips a year back to Chicago to hand deliver wine to my former boss. That little black case holds six bottles of wine.

"So, that is the story about Vinnie, the hit man."

None of the gang knew what to say. Flash looked at Fuzzy and noticed she was crying.

After a long pause, Bugs said, "Mr. Vinnie, we really were a bunch of nosy kids, and I know we are all sorry for thinking you might be a hit man."

Vinnie laughed and replied, "Oh, think nothing of it. Like I said, I am a loner right now, so it doesn't matter what some people might think of me, as long as I am not what they think. I am not looking for sympathy, so I am asking all of you to keep our little meeting just between us. But remember, don't jump to conclusions and don't gossip about somebody just because they happen to be a little different. And Fuzzy and Flash, let this one incident of breaking and entry be the only one in which you two are ever again involved."

Flash said, "Don't worry, Vinnie, I've learned my lesson."

"So have I," added Fuzzy.

"I have one more thing to talk about. This is for all of you." Vinnie made eye contact with each of them. They realized that Vinnie had reverted to a teacher and was teaching them.

"When things in your life seem almost too much to handle, remember this story about a large mayonnaise jar and two cups of coffee."

Vinnie placed a gallon mayonnaise jar on the table and filled it with golf balls. "Now, tell me, is the jar full?"

Foxtail responded, "It sure looks full to me."

"Ah, but it is not entirely full." Vinnie then picked up a box of pebbles and poured them into the jar. They rattled down between and around the golf balls until all of them were inside the jar. "Now is the jar full?"

Nobody ventured an answer this time.

"No, it is still not entirely full, because I can still pour this entire box of sand into the jar. He poured the sand into the jar, and it filled the empty spaces between the golf balls and the pebbles. "Now, is the jar full?"

Flash ventured an answer. "I think it is full now."

"It would seem so, but I can still pour two cups of coffee into the jar."

Vinnie poured the coffee into the jar.

"This mayonnaise jar represents your life. The golf balls represent important things: your spirituality, your family, your children, your health and your friends. The pebbles are the other things that matter like your job, your home and your possessions. The sand is everything else, the small stuff.

"If you fill the jar with sand first, there is no room for the golf balls or the pebbles. The same goes for life. If you spend all your time and energy on small stuff, you'll never have room for the things that are important.

"Take care of the golf balls and the pebbles first; the rest is just sand.

"Oh, yes, the coffee. No matter how full your life may be, there is always room for a couple of cups of coffee with a friend."

As the kids were leaving, Fuzzy motioned for Vinnie to bend over to her level. She turned her head up to his ear, cupped her hands and softly said, "I like coffee. I wouldn't mind coming over some time and having a couple of cups with you."

He put his arms around her, hugged her and leaned down to whisper, "I wouldn't mind that either."

The Dead Giveaway

THE DEPUTY SHERIFF, Ron Frisbie, was driving along a county road, heading toward Owappaho, when two boys appeared in the middle of the road. They were frantically waving their arms for him to stop. He recognized Squarehead and Knuckles. He pulled over the shoulder of the road, stopped and got out as the two boys came running up to his patrol car.

"Hey, what's the problem, boys? You act like you've seen a ghost."

The larger of the two boys, Knuckles, said, "Oh, It's worser than that, Ron; it's a lot worser than that. We just found a dead body down there in the river."

Squarehead added, "We was fishing when my hook got caught on something. I thought it was a snag on some brush, but when I started reeling it in toward me, I thought I was going to bust my line. Even thought it might be a big snapper, 'cause sometimes they don't fight like a fish, but when I got up to the bank, I seen it was a person."

Knuckles said, "It's a person all right; it's a dead person, and it looks like a woman."

The deputy picked up his microphone and called in. "Sally, this is Ron. Tell the sheriff I have just been stopped by a couple of boys, down here about three miles south of town, who tell me they have found a body in the river. I am going down to investigate. I'll get back with you as soon as I know anything."

He turned to the boys. "Okay, boys, show me what you have found."

They turned down toward the river. The area was thick with small tree saplings and tall weeds. The deputy had somewhat of a struggle getting through the thick growth as he followed the boys down the slope. When they reached the river, the ground flattened out into a gravel bar. Just beyond the gravel bar was a deep hole in which the boys had been fishing. The deputy approached the edge of the water and discovered the boys knew what they were talking about.

He told the boys he was proud of them for reporting what they had found. Ron knew how to contact the boys later because he was also their scoutmaster. He told the boys to go on home; they didn't need a second invitation. The deputy made sure the body couldn't be pulled back into the deep water by the current. Then he went back to the patrol car and called in his report.

"Sally, you better tell Jack to contact the coroner and come on out here. The boys were right; there is a female body out here."

He noted in his report it was 10:15 a.m. He didn't have to wait long before Sheriff Jack Carson and the coroner were on the scene.

Knuckles and Squarehead didn't go on home as they had indicated they would do, but instead they were hiding behind a patch of cattails and observing the action.

As they were pulling the body from the river, the sheriff said, "I don't know about you guys, but I recognize this woman."

Squarehead whispered, "I can see bullet holes from here."

The coroner, who was a crusty old geezer, said, "I recognize her, too; this is Chuck Gooding's wife."

When Knuckles heard them mention Chuck Gooding, he said, "Let's hightail it back to town and go hide over by Chuck's house. There ought to be some real action there." They sneaked back up to the road and took off running.

Deputy Frisbee asked the sheriff, "Jack, didn't Chuck tell us a week or so ago that his wife had left him and gone back to Georgia?"

The sheriff answered, "He sure did. But this sure puts a different spin on things."

While discussing the case on the way back to town, the sheriff and his deputy agreed they had seen at least three bullet holes in the body. The sheriff continued, "I guess we will just have to wait for the coroner's report. In the meantime, I have the honor of telling Chuck."

Ron said, "I just cannot believe Chuck killed her."

Jack added, "He has a hell of a temper, but I think you're right. He damn near wrecked his car one time trying to keep from running over a turtle. I can't believe he could ever hurt her. But, like I say, he does have a temper, and he did say she had left him."

The sheriff sat quiet for a moment before saying, "Wouldn't this just frost your gonads? Here I am less than a year from retiring, and I have a dad-blasted murder case to solve."

They drove directly to Gooding's house. Chuck opened the door before they were halfway up the sidewalk. "What the hell are you guys doing here? I know I've had a couple of traffic tickets, and I beat the crap out of Bob Graves last week, but I didn't think I had done anything that would take both of you to handle."

The sheriff said, "Chuck, there just isn't no delicate way of telling you this, except saying it right out; your wife has been murdered. We found her body in the river this morning."

Hiding around the corner of Chuck's house, the boys could hear everything that was going on. They could see Chuck as he stopped in his tracks and got a look like he had been struck by a thunderbolt.

Chuck made a little nervous chuckle, as he said, "Jack, this ain't nothing to be joshing around about. Are you guys sure it is her?"

"It's her, Chuck."

He grabbed his head with both hands and just wilted down on his hunkers.

They took Chuck back in the house where they sat down at the kitchen table. Chuck told them about a note his wife had left in the typewriter. He stood up, "Hell, I still have the note. I saved it,"

The two boys had moved up under the kitchen window where they could hear what was being said.

Chuck turned and went into another room where he retrieved a sheet of paper and brought it to the sheriff. "Here is the note she left me."

The note read: "I have had it with you. I cannot take it one more day. I am going to Georgia, and I am not coming back. Sharon."

The sheriff said, "Chuck, this note could have been typed by anyone."

"Jack, you do remember me telling you and Ron about her leaving me?'

The sheriff answered, "Yes, I remember." The deputy nodded, indicating he remembered.

Chuck told them about the troubles he and Sharon had been having. "We should have split up long ago. I tried to get along with her and ignore her faults. We never should have gotten together in the first place."

Ron asked, "How long were you two married?"

"Well, It'll come out sooner or later, so I just as well tell you now. We never were married."

Knuckles whispered, "Mom is right. She said there was something fishy about Chuck's wife."

"Okay, how long have you lived together?"

"We've been together six years. The truth of the matter is, she never got a divorce from her last husband; that's why we couldn't get married."

The sheriff stood up. "Chuck, just make sure you don't go anywhere."

"I won't even leave town, Sheriff."

As they started to leave, the sheriff turned and asked, "Do you own a gun?"

Chuck answered, "Yes. I have a shotgun for hunting, and I have a small 25 mm automatic pistol."

The sheriff told Chuck to get the pistol. He turned and reached up on the top of a kitchen cabinet, felt around for a moment and brought his hand down with a small leather holster, but no pistol.

He got a surprised look in his eyes. "It's gone."

Ron asked, "How long has it been since you saw it?"

Chuck thought for a moment before answering, "I really can't recall the last time I saw it. All I know, is that is where I kept it."

"What kind was it?"

"It was a Sterling Automatic. I remember when I bought it at a second-hand store, I remarked it might be sterling, but it sure wasn't silver."

"Did you keep it loaded?"

"I kept the clip loaded, but I never had a bullet in the chamber."

"Did Sharon know where you kept it?"

"Yes, she did. But I can't think she took it with her. Hell, she had so many clothes, I can't even tell if she took any of them."

Squarehead whispered, "We better get out of here before someone sees us."

They were out of sight by the time the sheriff and the deputy left Chuck's home.

Two days later the coroner's report was on the sheriff's desk. It indicated the body had died of a broken neck before it was dumped in the river, and that it had been shot six times with a 25 mm weapon. Four bullets had been retrieved from the body.

The sheriff told his deputy, "Let's not mention the actual cause of death, for now. That is between you and me and the coroner."

A second report, compiled by two detectives, indicated a 25mm Sterling Automatic Pistol had been found in the shallow water, upstream one mile from where the body was found.

The sheriff had all he needed to charge Chuck Gooding with the murder of his wife. He ordered Deputy Frisbee, "Pick him up."

Knuckles saw the police car pull to a stop in front of Chuck's house, so he called Squarehead. "Get over here right now. They are arresting Chuck. We need to get down to the jail."

Squarehead answered, "I'll meet you there."

When Ron arrived at the jail with Chuck, the sheriff produced the automatic the detectives had found and asked, "Is this your pistol?"

Chuck took only a slight glance before he immediately recognized the small weapon. "It sure looks like mine, Jack. I don't know how in the hell it got here, but I think it is mine. Did it have any prints on it?"

"Not a smudge. Now we will have to wait for the ballistics report before we know for sure if it is the weapon matches the bullets found in the body."

The sheriff leaned across his desk and looked Chuck square in the eye for a moment. "Chuck, is there anything you know that you have not told me?"

The two boys had slipped into the restroom in the hallway between the sheriff's office and the dispatcher's office; they left the door partly open so they could hear.

"The only thing I know that could possibly be of help is this." He extended his right hand forward with his palm down. "See those two little scars between my thumb knuckle and my pointing finger knuckle?"

"What are you getting at, Chuck?"

"I got those two scars on my hand the first few times I ever fired that little 25 automatic."

"And?"

"If you have a big hand like mine, and you fire that little Sterling without holding it right, the bolt will scrape the hell out of your hand as it comes back and then goes forward to throw another round in the chamber. I fired it three different times before I realized how to hold it so it wouldn't peel the hide off my hand."

The sheriff sat motionless for a moment. Then he sat down and said, "Okay."

Chuck added, "All I know for sure is I did not kill Sharon. If someone stole that little pistol and shot her with it, and they were not familiar with the proper way to grip it, they could have scars on their hand just like I do."

Knuckles whispered, "Hey, Squarehead, have you noticed that Fred Snyder has his left hand bandaged?"

"Yeah, I was in the bank with Mom this morning, and he does have his hand bandaged. And he is left-handed."

Knuckles continued, "That guy is supposed to be one of the town's best guys. He goes to church every Sunday and all that stuff. Boy, he would do anything to cover it up if he was messing around with some other woman, other than his wife."

They heard the sheriff say, "Sorry, Chuck, but we are going to have to lock you up for now."

The two boys hurried out the back door and went over to the library. They asked the librarian for a sheet of paper on which they wrote, "TELL JACK TO CHECK FRED SNYDER'S LEFT HAND. Signed: Knuckles and Squarehead."

They then went out behind the jail and up to the cell window. They wrapped the sheet of paper around a rock, threw it through the open cell window and ran for home.

Chuck jumped as the rock hit the floor in front of his feet, "What the hell!"

He picked up the rock and removed the paper. After reading the note, he called for the sheriff.

The sheriff came to the cell door. "Now what?"

"Read this."

"Where did you get this note? And who in the hell are Knuckles and Squarehead?"

Deputy Frisbee never said a word; he just smiled. Then he asked, "Jack, have you noticed that Fred does have his hand bandaged?"

"As a matter of fact, I have."

"Why don't you guys wait until he takes that bandage off, and then check his hand? I never thought about him, but I thought I saw him leaving my house one night as I was coming home. Then another time earlier, he was there, but Sharon said he was returning her purse that she left at the bank."

Two days later deputy Frisbee noticed the bandage was gone. He told the sheriff, and the sheriff called the bank. He was aware that Fred was a collector of confederate coins.

"Hey, Fred, could you come over to my office? There is a guy in here with a box of old confederate money; I'll bet you would like you to look at."

"Oh, you bet I would. I'll be right over."

Within three minutes, Fred walked into the sheriff's office.

"Let me see your left hand, Fred."

"Why do you want to see my hand?'

"Never mind, just put it down on the desk, right here."

Fred looked puzzled, but he placed his hand on the sheriff's desk.

"Palm down, please."

"What's going on here, Jack?"

The deputy stepped forward, grasped Fred's hand and turned it palm down.

"Where did you get those two fresh scars."

Fred was no dummy; he knew instantly he had been caught. There could be no other reason for the confederate money deception. He slowly sat down in a chair by the desk.

"We lifted your prints from a coffee cup at the café; they matched the ones on the holster you tossed back on top of that kitchen cabinet."

Fred put his head down on folded arms on the sheriff's desk and started to weep.

Later in the day, Fred told of how he was having an affair with Sharon. He wanted to break it off and she became very angry. She got up on a chair and got that gun. As she tried to remove it from the holster, she dropped the gun. Fred grabbed the holster from her and tossed it back on top the cabinet. He then picked up the gun and put it into his pocket. She became violent and started screaming and hitting him. In the heat of the moment, he grabbed her around the neck and gave her head a quick twist. She fell in a heap.

Fred tried to revive her, but could not. He hurriedly carried her out to his car and tossed her in the back seat. He drove out to the bridge and tossed her body in the water. As she floated to the surface, he took the pistol from his pocket and emptied it into her body. He told them he thought she was already dead, but he shot her for good measure. Then he wiped the gun clean and tossed it in the river.

When he got in the car, he discovered his left hand had been cut pretty badly with the bolt of that little gun. He bandaged it himself and later told his wife he pinched it real bad with the car hood.

When Chuck was released, Deputy Frisbee told him, "Squarehead is Jimmie Oplotmic, and Knuckles is Gus Palmer."

"You don't say? Guess I'm going to have to give those boys a commendation. I think we would have solved this case eventually, but their note sure helped it along."

Let's Talk About God

IT WAS JUST another warm summer day. Fuzzy and the boys were gathered in the small shelter house at the little park, just hanging out. They talked about getting up a game of work-up, and then one of the boys suggested they all go skinny-dipping at the razor pit.

Fuzzy squelched that idea with, "Now, listen here, you turkeys, you know I can't go skinny-dipping with you guys out at the razor pit or anywhere else. It ain't that it would bother me none; I just don't want folks telling around that I'm a slut."

"Fuzzy, you are the cussingest girl I ever heard of."

"Hey, Squarehead, it wouldn't hurt you to cuss a little once in awhile."

"I don't want God to be making a list against me."

"Oh, poof, God ain't got time to go around making lists about kids cussing."

"How do you know he ain't, Fuzzy?"

"I don't know, and I don't give a shit. I just know if I was God I would have lots more important things to do than making lists of cuss words people use."

"There you go again, using even a worse word."

"Oh, bull, Squarehead, there are a lot worse cussing words than slut and shit."

Bugs entered the conversation. "Squarehead, you're a Catholic, ain't you?"

"Yes, and I have to go to confession at least once a month and tell Father O'Conner about anything I've done wrong."

Flash asked, "What do you do if you ain't done nothing wrong?"

"Oh, there is usually something I have done bad; I ain't no angel, after all."

Fuzzy put in, "Well, I ain't known you a very long time, but I don't remember you ever doing anything wrong."

Squarehead continued, "One thing for sure, Fuzzy, if you was Catholic, you would have to carry a notebook and a pencil with you all the time; and you would be getting writer's cramps, just writing down the cuss words you say."

Fuzzy remarked, "Now let's see. There are ten commandments, ain't they? But I don't remember any of them saying anything about, 'Thou shalt not cuss.' "

"There's one that says, "Thou shalt not use the name of the Lord in vain."

"That don't say nothing about cussing. Besides, I don't use the name of the Lord in my cussing."

Squarehead looked Fuzzy straight in the eyes and asked, "Fuzzy, do you believe in God?"

"I don't really know what to believe. I know that all the stuff in the world and out in the sky, with all those stars and stuff, had to come from somewhere. Somebody had to start the world and put the people in it, but how in the hell does anybody expect a kid to know about all that? Maybe God did do it. The Bible says he did, and that he did it all in six days, and then rested a day. Sounds pretty impossible to me, but what the hell? Since I don't know any better answer, I'll go along with the idea that God did it all."

"Fuzzy, do you believe in Jesus?" Squarehead asked.

"Yeah, I can see that a nice guy like Jesus could have lived here a long time ago. He must have, because everybody seems to know about him. I can go along with that. The Bible has all kinds of stories about Jesus being a real person, but most of the time when they mention God, He is just a voice coming out of a rock or a bush or something."

"Fuzzy, How did you know about God's voice coming out of a bush or a rock?" asked Bugs.

"Hey, guys, we might not go every Sunday, but me and Grandpa Frank go to church sometimes. And if the preacher can tell something interesting enough to keep us awake, we might even go three or four weeks in a row."

Bugs asked, "Do any of you guys ever read the Bible?"

Foxtail answered, "I have tried to read the Bible, but I just don't understand it. It's too complicated for me. I just have to let the preachers tell me about it."

Fuzzy spoke up, "Huh, what if the preacher is like the one Grandpa Tivitts was talking about the other day?"

Flash spoke up, "What did my grandpa tell you about some preacher?"

"He didn't tell it to me exactly, I just heard him telling John Barns about it."

"Did he know you was listening?"

"No, Flash, he didn't even know I was there."

"What did he say?"

"He said Preacher Bayers was a pinhead, and that if brains was vinegar, he wouldn't have enough to pickle a rat turd."

Bugs started laughing. "Grandpa Tivitts said that? That's funny."

Fuzzy added, "Of course, he said it. I wouldn't say he said it if he didn't say it. He says lots of funny stuff like that."

"Yes, and Grandma fusses at him about it, too, and she says he encourages you."

"Oh, poof, Flash, he don't encourage me; I don't need no encouragement. But let's get back to talking about God."

Flash said, "We was talking about the Bible. My grandma reads the Bible almost every day. And she reads Bible stories to me. Then we talk about them. Some of them are pretty interesting, ain't they, Fuzzy?' You've heard her tell some."

"Yeah, they are when she tells them; but almost everything she tells about is interesting. Same way with Grandpa; I bet if Grandpa Tivitts was a preacher, that church would be full of people every Sunday."

Knuckles hadn't entered the conversation until he said, "You know something, guys, I started believing in God one late evening when I was out in a corn field listening to the corn grow."

"Listening to the corn grow?" Fuzzy blurted, "If that wouldn't sugar your cookies. That must have been exciting. How did you keep from having a heart attack?"

"Just let me talk, Fuzzy. This ain't funny; it's serious. Did you ever stop to think about how a little bitty grain of corn, that's all shriveled up and dried out, can be planted in the ground, and then within a few months there is a big tall stalk of corn growed right up out of that little seed?"

"And that made you start believing in God?"

"How else can you explain something like that, guys?"

"But you said you were listening to the corn grow."

"Yes, I did. I found out that if you go out in the cornfield in the late evening, or even after dark, when the wind ain't blowing and everything is still and quiet. And just sit down and be real quiet, you can hear the corn grow."

The ever-skeptical Fuzzy said, "Oh, bull, Knuckles, corn can't talk."

"I didn't say I heard it talk, I said I could hear it grow. It makes little squeaky sounds, and sometimes it pops, like my knuckles pop, only not as loud."

"You are serious, ain't you?" Bugs said.

"Yes, I'm serious. I think the corn plant must suck up water at night as it grows from the inside out. And as the corn stalk gets taller and fatter, the leaves that wrap around the stalk where they come off it sort of squeak and pop as they slip when the stalk gets fatter."

Flash added, "You know something, guys? What he says makes sense. Have you ever noticed how fast corn grows? One day it will be five inches tall, and before you know it, it will be five feet tall."

No one said anything for a moment, as they were all thinking about what Knuckles had said. Then Fuzzy spoke up. "Knuckles, you have said something that has made me start thinking. It's almost like a miracle the way a plant of any kind can start out as a little tiny seed, and then grow up to be as big as even a tree. Every weed, every tree, every plant of any kind starts out from a little dinky shriveled-up, dried-out seed. Maybe it is God that makes all that possible. I still don't understand it, and I don't think I ever will."

Flash went on to say, "My grandma says that God is everywhere at all times. She says the spirit of God is in every living thing. He is also a part of the trees, the ground, the water and even the air."

Fuzzy added, "You guys know I am part Indian, and what he just told about what Grandma said is what Indians believe. Grandpa Frank told me they believe in the 'Great Spirit,' so, since I am part Indian, I guess it is built right in me. That's what I believe. And if you ever heard an Indian talk, you couldn't tell if he was praying or cussing."

"You know that little community church over near Owappaho is going to have Bible school this summer; maybe we ought to all go to it. It just lasts one week."

"I don't know, Bugs. Would they let a Catholic go to a protestant Bible school?"

"Oh, hell, yes, they would, Squarehead. It's a community church; they don't care who comes as long as they drop something in the collection plate."

"That ain't true, Fuzzy. You don't have to have any money for the collection plate." Foxtail remarked, "I don't think there is any church anywhere that turns people away if they're broke."

Fuzzy stood up and stretched. "I don't know about you guys, but I am willing to go to Bible school for a week if any of the rest of you want to go."

Bugs said, "Let's vote on it. All in favor, let it be known by the usual sign of a gang vote." He counted the hands. "Well, it looks like it's unanimous. We'll go."

Fuzzy spoke up, "I have had enough religion for today. Let's talk politics. Grandpa Frank says he is like Will Rogers, whoever that is. Grandpa Frank says he don't belong to any organized political party; he's a Democrat."

Jake the Snake

ONE EVENING, WHEN Flash, Fuzzy, Bugs and Knuckles were sitting on grandpa Tivitts' front porch, they looked up to see on old man hobbling up the road. He was walking slowly and supporting himself with a crooked walking stick that looked a lot like a big stiff black snake.

Fuzzy pointed in the direction of the old man, "Grandpa, who is that old geezer? I was with Grandpa Frank in the grocery store in Owappaho the other day and he was in there buying stuff. He stunk like an old billy goat, and he was breathing like a wind-broken horse. I'll bet he ain't had a haircut or a shave or a bath in a coon's age."

"How does a wind-broken horse breathe?" asked Flash.

"Like this." Fuzzy proceeded to make some wheezing growling sounds.

"Hell, he sounds like a chainsaw," she added.

Grandpa said, "I don't know much about him. All I know is he showed up around here a month or so ago, that he has had several confrontations with people, and with the law. I have heard he lives about a mile out of town in an old abandoned derailed boxcar that was left on that switch track to the mine when they took tracks out. He just moved in and took it over. The sheriff told him to move, but he just pays no attention to him"

"You mean that old boxcar away

over there by that big tailing pile?" Bugs asked.

"Yeah, that's the place. And there is also a dugout under that tailing pile, right next to the old boxcar, where the mine owner used to store his dynamite. I never was in it, but I have heard it is about half as big as an average-sized room in a house."

Fuzzy added, "The way he stinks, I'll bet he ain't even got water to wash his face with out there. He looks like a picture of life's other side, slowly fading away."

"Some people call him "Jake the Snake" because of that crooked walking stick he always has with him. I have been told he is a real mean, so you kids stay away from him."

"Don't worry about me," Fuzzy added. "I got enough of him at the grocery store. He is ugly as home-made sin, he has one eye out and if my poop smelled as bad as his breath, I'd drown myself."

Grandpa chuckled and said, "Fuzzy, my Lord, child, that is one expression you never got from me."

"Nah, I just made that one up."

Later that evening when Grandma and Grandpa Tivitts were getting ready for bed, Grandpa said, "Did you hear the kids talking about that old fellow they call Jake the Snake?"

"No. I guess I wasn't listening. Why?"

"Jake the Snake is Darrell Hadley. Do you remember him?"

"Darrel Hadley. Hmmm. Oh, yeah, wasn't he the guy who was convicted of murder when you sat on that jury 20 years ago?"

"That is the same guy. Ed Barns told me he had been released from prison, but nobody knew where he went. But I recognized him as soon as I saw him. He has grown a beard and allowed his hair to get long in hopes no one will recognize him. But that old fart they call Jake the Snake is Darrell Hadley."

"Didn't his wife divorce him and move back east somewhere after he was convicted?"

"Yes. As you recall, it was one of her brothers that he killed."

"Are you going to tell the kids about him?"

"I don't know what to do. I sure as hell don't want them hanging around him."

"Well, Owen, let's sleep on it."

Little did the kids realize that before the week was out they would all get much better acquainted with Jake the Snake.

Grandma told Flash she would bake a nice blackberry pie if she had some berries. She mentioned there used to be a big patch of berries over by that old abandoned railroad track about a mile north of Camp 4. So he asked Fuzzy to go investigate with him. When they arrived at the patch, they found the bushes were loaded with big fat, juicy berries.

Fuzzy tasted a few berries and then said, "Hey, you know what? Let's get the whole gang together and pick all these berries before they fall off the vines. Why, I'll bet there are enough berries here to make a hundred pies. Just look at those bushes; they are on both sides of this old right-of-way as far as I can see. We can pick them and sell them."

Within less than an hour, Fuzzy and the five boys were at the west end of the berry bushes, three on one side of the old right-of-way and three on the other side. Each on of them had a bucket as they worked their way south through the patch. They were all laughing and visiting as they picked the berries.

"Hey, Knuckles, I think you are eating more than you are putting in the bucket. Don't you know too many berries all at once will give you the back alley quick step?" Fuzzy remarked.

"What's the back alley quick step?"

"The runs, Flash, the runs. And don't ask what the runs are."

"I think I know what the runs are, Fuzzy."

Since all the kids were working their way east, they were not paying attention to a storm cloud that was building up to the west of them; it was upon them before they had time to even think about it.

All at once the clouds opened up and the rain came down in sheets. They were also not paying attention to how close they were getting to Jake the Snake's boxcar.

Suddenly they heard a voice calling, "For God's sake, kids! Look behind you. There is a tornado on the ground, and it is heading straight in this direction."

Fuzzy yelled, "Holy shit. Look at the tail on that sucker!"

Jake was yelling, "Come here, you crazy little rug rats. Get your butts in my dugout!"

They didn't have time to think. They could see the debris flying in the air as the elephantine trunk of the tornado was weaving its way across a field and coming straight toward their location.

Jake was yelling, "Come on! Come on! Hurry, get in here before you all get killed!" He was motioning from an opening in the side of the tailing pile that was about four feet wide and six feet high.

They all hurried through the pouring rain and into the dugout just as the tornado hit the railroad car in which Jake the Snake lived. They watched the railroad car disintegrate before their eyes.

Bugs said, "I don't think it hit Camp 4 or Owappaho. It looked like it was just going across an open field."

Foxtail remarked, "I'll bet that thing sucked all the crawdads right out of their holes."

Fuzzy added, "Well, it sure as hell sucked that boxcar out of its hole. There ain't nothing left of it, except those big iron wheels."

She started to leave the dugout, but as she attempted to go past Jake the Snake, he put an arm out and stopped her.

"Get your hands off me, you stinking old bastard. I'm going home to see if Grandpa Frank is okay."

"Do as you wish, young lady, but I think you should take a look at the size of those hailstones before you venture out."

A look to the west revealed a wall of hailstones approaching the dugout opening. Some of them were hitting the ground and bouncing through the opening to where they were all standing.

Foxtail reached down and picked up a large chunk of hail. "Wow! Look at the size of this thing. Fuzzy, if that would have hit you in the head, it would have killed you."

She turned to the old man. "Thanks for keeping me from going out, mister. I'm sorry I cussed you."

He didn't answer; he just wilted down on an empty wooden box that was near the opening, lowered his head and placed his right hand on his forehead. "Oh, Lord, I didn't have much, but now I have lost it all." Then he turned his face upward and continued through labored breathing, "Dear God, thank you for sparing these kids. I am so thankful this dugout shelter was here."

The rain continued to come down in sheets as the six kids stood and looked out the dugout door over the slumped figure of the much-feared Jake the Snake.

Squarehead was the first to say anything as he moved up to the old man, placed a hand on his shoulder and said, "I'm sure sorry you lost your home, mister. And I'm also very happy that you hollered at us kids in time. We sure would have been gonners."

"It's okay, son. The main thing is that you are all still okay."

Squarehead continued, "Do you have a name besides Jake the Snake?"

"Jake the Snake? Where in the world did you get that?"

"I guess everybody calls you that because you have that crooked walking stick that looks like a big stiff black snake," Bugs remarked.

"Huh? Well, I guess that makes sense."

"Do you have a name?"

"Of course, I have a name, young lady. Everybody has a name, but I doubt that anyone around here gives a darn what my name might be."

"I do, and so do the boys. Don't you, guys?"

"Do all of you kids have names?"

"Yeah. I'm Fuzzy; he's Bugs; he's Foxtail; that's Knuckles; there's Flash, and he is Squarehead." She pointed them all out to the old man.

"Those names must surely be nicknames. I have never heard an assortment of names to compare with you kids."

"Yeah, they are nicknames. But you ain't told us what to call you."

"I kind of like Jake the Snake. Guess I'll be just plain old 'Jake.'"

The rain was beginning to stop and the sky was clearing in the west. The tornado was one of those rare occasions when a thunderstorm turns bad all at once. It had developed only a mile or so west of where the kids were picking berries, and it dissipated not long after it destroyed the boxcar.

All the kids thanked Jake for saving them from the storm and headed back to where they dropped their berry buckets. Only two buckets were to be found, and the berry bushes were stripped clean by the hail.

Bugs looked around and remarked, "Well, I guess that puts an end to our blackberry money-making project."

Flash added, "Yeah, and we didn't even get enough berries to make a single pie."

Squarehead looked back toward the spot where the boxcar once stood. "You know what? I think everybody is wrong about old Jake. I'll bet he ain't near as mean as he looks."

"He sure as hell looks mean. If he had a patch over that bad eye and a knife in his teeth, he would look as mean as them story book pirates," Fuzzy added.

Squarehead continued, "But he wasn't mean to us. He even thanked the Lord that he had a place for us to hide in. That don't sound very mean."

They all agreed with Squarehead. Then they shuffled along through the wet grass as they headed back to the Tivitts' house.

Again, it was Squarehead who seemed to be most affected by the encounter with Jake the Snake. He continued, "All he has to live in now is that hole in the side of the tailing pile, and it don't even have a door on it."

Fuzzy spoke up, "What do you think we can do about it? Hell, I bet he don't even know how to live like a normal person."

"How do we know he don't, Fuzzy? Maybe he is just a guy who ain't had nothing but bad luck. That tornado didn't seem to do any damage anywhere else but at Jake's boxcar."

Knuckles agreed. "You're right, Squarehead. He helped us, so maybe we should do something to help him."

Bugs stopped and held his hand up for the rest to stop. "You guys know something? There is an empty house way over to the south edge of Camp 4 that hasn't been lived in as long as I can remember. It sure ain't much, but it is as good as that boxcar was, I bet."

Foxtail added, "Yeah, I know where it is. You can't even see it now for the horseweeds and the tree sprouts. The termites have probably chewed it up pretty bad, but I know it has a good well by the house. One real dry summer, my dad and I went there and got water for our tomato plants."

The kids had reached the Tivitts' home where they found Grandma and Grandpa and Grandpa Frank sitting on the porch.

Grandma said, "Did you kids get caught in that quick thundershower about an hour ago?"

"Hey, Grandma, you must not have been looking north. That was more'n any damn thundershower; that thing had an elephant trunk that just tore hell out of Jake the Snake's place."

"What are you talking about, Fuzzy?"

Flash spoke up, "Oh, Grandma, it was a tornado all right. We were picking berries and didn't see it coming until we heard Jake yelling at us to take cover in his dugout."

"Whoa! Wait a minute." Grandpa jumped to his feet. "You had to take cover in Jake's dugout. What the hell were you doing over there? I told you kids to stay away from him."

"The berry picking was so good that we weren't paying attention to how close we were getting to Jake's. And then when he yelled at us and we looked up at that thing, we didn't have time to do anything else. And another thing: he kept me from running out in the hail storm and getting the crap knocked out of me."

"Hail storm?" He turned to Granny and Frank, "Where were we when all this took place? We had a quick rain shower for a few minutes, but we didn't have any hail; and for sure we didn't have a tornado."

Squarehead stepped forward. "Mr. Tivitts, Jake ain't really mean. He was good to us. And now he don't have his boxcar anymore, and we were wondering if we could help him get moved into that abandoned house over south of town."

"Just a minute, Squarehead. You kids are saying that a tornado has destroyed the boxcar that old man lives in?"

"Yes" ... "Uh huh" ... "It sure did" ... "That's exactly what we're saying."

"And now you are wanting to help him move into that old abandoned house south of town?"

"That's the least we can do" ... "Yep" ... "We sure are" ... "Sounds like a good plan to me."

"What does the old man say about it?"

Fuzzy spoke up, "Oh, he don't know nothing about it. We were talking about it after we left his place."

"Kids, that is a noble idea. But you kids know absolutely nothing about Jake the Snake. I know about that house. It belonged to an elderly couple at one time. When they passed on, there was no record of relatives, so it now belongs to the county, much like a number of other abandoned houses in these old mine camps."

"What is the county going to do with it?"

"I guess the same thing they have been doing with for the past 20 years — nothing."

Squarehead said, "Then Jake moving into that old house wouldn't be much different than when he moved into that boxcar."

"Not exactly, son, the boxcar belonged to the railroad company, and they tried to get the old man to leave. I guess they decided it wasn't worth the hassle."

"Great! I'm going back out there and tell him what we want to do."

Bugs added, "Okay, Squarehead, you go talk to him, and the rest of us will go take a look at that old house. Come on, gang, let's roll."

Grandpa spoke up, "If you go back out there, I am going with you. I need to have a talk with that gentleman."

When Squarehead and Grandpa Tivitts approached the opening of the dugout, they observed the old man still sitting on that wooden box, but this time he had a framed picture in his hands. He was holding the picture against his heart, looking up with his eyes closed.

Squarehead was hesitant to approach the dugout as he could tell the old man was deep thought. But Owen Tivitts was not. He told Squarehead to wait until he had talked to Jake, and then he walked right up to the man.

The old man jumped and gasped a little.

"I'm sorry, I didn't mean to scare you."

"It's okay. What do you want?"

"Do you remember me?"

Jake rose to his feet and took a good look before answering, "Yes, you are Owen Tivitts. I remember you well. You were on the jury that convicted me. And before you say another word, I want you to know the jury was right in that decision. I have been hoping I would run into some of you and actually thank you."

"Is that right? You mean you are not unhappy that I helped put you away for 20 years?"

"Not at all, Owen. I didn't intend to kill my brother-in-law, but I did it in a fit of anger and I needed to pay for it. I learned a lot in prison."

Squarehead stepped up to the two men and said, "I see you found a picture. Did you find anything else?"

"Most of what I had were books and letters and records, the kind of things that could not survive a storm like that one. Apparently, I lost everything. But I had this picture in the dugout." He held it up for Squarehead to see.

"Is that you and your family?"

"What is your name, son?"

"I'm James Oplotski, but everyone calls me Squarehead."

"This is a picture of my family and me. It was taken during happier days."

"I can tell that it is you, even if you don't have whiskers in the picture. I can tell by your eyes.

Jake sighed heavily. "That was many years ago. Now, James, what may I do for you and Mr. Tivitts?"

"It ain't what you can do for us; it's what we can do for you."

"What are you getting at?"

"There is a house here in Camp 4 that ain't been lived in for a long, long time. It don't belong to anybody, unless you count the county. And me and the other kids would like to clean up all the weeds and brush around it and fix it up for you to live in."

The old man was speechless. He sat motionless for a full minute before he responded. "Wait a minute, son. You are telling me there is a house here into which I might move, that it belongs to the county?"

"Yep. That's what I am saying."

"And you kids want to do that for me?" He breathed heavily for a moment. "What do you think of that Owen?"

"Squarehead, would you go on back to the house, I need to talk to Jake in private for awhile."

As Squarehead left, Owen looked at Jake and said, "Just say it's okay for us to do it, and we'll start cleaning it up."

With the boy gone, Owen said, "You are telling me that 20 years in prison was good for you. How can I be sure about that?"

"I guess you can't be sure about it until I have had a chance to prove myself. I have checked around the community, and I find you are the only one still living here that knew anything about me."

"You sound sincere enough."

"Owen, I have lost my family over what I did, and I have no hopes of ever getting them back. It is probably just as well, because I certainly was not a husband or a father. I took a lot of beatings during the first five years I was in prison. I have lost an eye, developed breathing problems, and I am crippled by arthritis, but I have educated myself. Believe it on not, I have a BS degree in history. And I also have a Divinity Degree. Even with that degree, I realize I am not cut out to be a preacher. I have to admit that I still have difficulty with certain swear words, but I'm working on that, too."

Owen was impressed, and he told the man so.

"I would just as soon keep on being known as Jake the Snake. I hope that I have enough remaining time in my life to make a positive contribution somewhere. You can plainly see, Owen, I am not physically able to be much of a threat to anyone, even if I were inclined to do so. I cannot hold a job, but my earlier Social Security deductions have made me eligible for a minimum pension, so I manage to get by."

"Well, what do you think about the proposal these kids are making?"

"I'm, overwhelmed. I just do not know what to say."

In the meantime, Fuzzy, Flash, Foxtail, Bugs and Knuckles were weaving their way through the thicket of small trees and big weeds that surrounded the old house. They first went to the back porch and found it was about to fall apart. They could see a broken window next to the door; however, the door was still on its hinges and was in working condition.

They opened the door and entered the house. The door led into a small kitchen that was furnished with a small table and four chairs. There was a cupboard against one wall and a kitchen sink attached to another wall. The sink cabinet had an old pitcher pump and a small wood-burning cook stove was next to the sink Off the kitchen was a small room with shelves on one side and a window in the end; it had a door opening, but no door.

There was an arched doorway leading from the kitchen into a fairly large living room. The living room contained two wooden rocking chairs, a couple of small end tables, one oval-shaped lamp table by a window with a kerosene lamp on it, an old divan and a wood or coal-burning heating stove. The wallpaper had come loose in several places and was hanging down. There were still curtains and faded green window blinds on the windows.

The doors leading from the living room went into two small bedrooms, back to the kitchen and out on the front porch. Each bedroom had a full-sized wrought iron bed with slats and springs. One of the beds had a cotton mattress and two feather pillows.

Fuzzy was the first to say anything. "Holy horse feathers, this old house looks like a museum. I'm surprised somebody hasn't broke in here and stole all this stuff."

Knuckles said, "It's because this little town don't have no crooks."

Flash remarked, "I don't see any light fixtures or any wall plugs. Do you suppose they didn't have electricity?"

Bugs answered, "Nobody in town had electricity until they got that rural electrical thing going. These folks who lived here were long gone by then."

Fuzzy asked, "What do you think, guys? It looks like the biggest chore will be cutting weeds and sprouts out of the yard."

Foxtail added, "Yeah, and we will have to clean out that old well and get that pitcher pump working."

Fuzzy added, "And he won't care about how the walls look. We can just pull off all that loose wallpaper, sweep the place out and turn it over to him."

"Okay, now we go back and see what Grandpa and Squarehead found out," Bugs said, as he headed out the kitchen door.

Arriving at the Tivitts' home, they discovered Grandpa and Squarehead waiting in the porch swing as they bombarded them with, "What did you find out? Was he tickled about the idea?"

"Are we going ahead with our project?"

Grandpa held up a hand. "Hold on, kids. I want to talk to you about this project. All of you sit down here on the porch. I want to tell you something."

They all seated themselves, and Grandpa continued. "I want to tell you that Jake the Snake is a man who has had a very tough life. At one time he was a very mean and dangerous person."

Fuzzy spoke up. "Did you used to know him, Grandpa?"

"Yes, Fuzzy, I knew him about 20 years ago, but he is not the same man he was then. I do think he is a person who has earned a second chance, and I cannot think of a better way of giving him that chance, or of a better bunch of kids to start the project. All I am asking is that you take Jake for what he is right now, and that you don't even try to look into his past. Remember this: Yesterday is history; tomorrow is a mystery; today is a gift — that's why we call it the present."

Squarehead said, "Yeah — today is a gift, so let's give old Jake a present."

The next day, Fuzzy and the boys were at the house before eight o'clock with axes, hand scythes and brush cutters. They were just getting started cutting weeds when two pickups stopped by the house. The pickups were followed by a panel truck with ladders. Then three cars pulled to a stop, and people began pouring out of the vehicles with scrubbing buckets, brooms, paintbrushes and wallpaper.

Fuzzy looked up and said, "What the hell is going on here?"

Grandpa stepped forward. "Well, kids, your idea has inspired the whole community. We are moving in here in force, and we are going to turn this house into community project. We are calling it, "Project Squarehead," because he was the main one of you kids who got the ball rolling.

Fuzzy yelled, "Yeee-Haaaa." And the boys all cheered.

Five days later, the walls were all papered and the woodwork painted. The roof was repaired, the broken windows replaced, the stove pipes replaced with new ones, the well cleaned and the pump fixed. The yard was cleared of all weeds and brush and the grass mowed; the outside toilet repaired and the coal shed repaired and a mailbox set up out by the road.

Owen had gone to Jake's dugout and prevailed upon him to come home with him. At the Tivitts' home, Jake took a bath and put on some of Grandpa's clean clothes. Grandma gave him a haircut and trimmed his beard and mustache; he looked like a new man. When he looked at himself in the mirror, he broke down and cried. He was even fitted with a proper eye patch. He could not believe there are so many wonderful people in this world.

Owen said, "Come on, Jake, Squarehead and his committee are here. They want to give you a personal escort to your new home."

Ketterman's Barn

ONE MILE NORTH and a quarter of a mile west of Camp 4 to the Coal Valley school crossroads stands a landmark that is also one of the more favorite hangouts for Fuzzy and her boys. At one point in its history, it was one of the most magnificent examples of Old German craftsmanship in the entire county. Old Man Ketterman's barn is still quite an imposing sight, because it stands alone on a hill that was once the sight of the Felix Ketterman homestead. The barn is the only example of sandstone construction in the area.

The barn was built to accommodate five teams of horses in five double stalls; it had a large tack room, four granaries and a huge hayloft. There was a walkway between the stalls and the granaries with a ladder at each end of the walkway as a means to climb up into the loft. Surrounding the barn was a stone fence corral. The farm complex also had several smaller buildings for sheep, hogs and chickens; there was a large smokehouse with a fruit cellar underneath, and the Ketterman family lived in a large two-story house that sat at the end of a long lane. It was a beautiful farmstead.

The Ketterman children are all grown and out on their own now. Mrs. Ketterman passed away several years ago, and Felix had lived alone in the big old house since he lost his wife.

It all came to an end one hot summer day when a Kansas tornado decided to pick the Ketterman place as a spot to wreak havoc. That day was also an example of how fickle a tornado can be; it destroyed the house, the sheep and hog barns, the chicken house, most of the many trees, and the smokehouse was picked up and slammed down into the storm cellar. Luckily, Mr. Ketterman was safe in a downstairs closet while the rest of the house was being ripped apart. Strangely, the huge barn sustained only minor damage from flying debris.

After the tornado did its damage, Mr. Ketterman took lath and plaster and finished the interior of the largest granary in the barn, making it like a room in a house. He lived in that granary until he had a house moved out from Camp 4. Now he uses that granary for a store room for the keepsakes that were protected by a closet when the house was destroyed,

Today, old man Ketterman now lives in that small house near the road at the end of the long lane that once led up the hill to the old farmstead. The barn stands alone at the top of the hill and is surrounded by a wheat field.

Once or twice a week, Mr. Ketterman will walk up the long lane to the barn, climb up into the hayloft and shoot free throws in the basketball goal he put up for recreational purposes. He is pretty good at this activity because his record is 34 straight; he tries to beat that record every time he goes out there.

One Saturday morning, Mr. Ketterman was outside his house early one morning when he thought he could hear a familiar sound of a basketball bouncing on his hayloft floor. He walked up the lane to the barn, quietly climbed the ladder leading to the loft until his eyes were level with the floor. There he saw a little skinny, fuzzy-headed girl shooting baskets with his basketball. He never said a word as he clung to the ladder and watched her with only his head protruding into the loft.

After a minute or so, the ball bounced off the goal and headed in his direction. When the little girl saw Mr. Ketterman, she jumped, stopped abruptly and said, "Who are you? You scared the shit out of me."

"The point is, who are you, young lady? And where did you come from?"

"I am Marvelle Thomas. I'm Frank Thomas' granddaughter."

He climbed on up in the loft. "Oh, so you are the little girl who is living with Frank? I have heard about you. Does he know where you are?"

"No. He's still sleeping."

"Do you roam around the country by yourself all the time?"

"No, most of the time I have my boys with me."

He chuckled. "Your boys? You have boys."

"Yeah. Five of them."

"Hmm. That's quite a few for a young girl. What are their names?"

"Well, there's Flash and Bugs and Foxtail and Knuckles and Squarehead; they call me Fuzzy."

He leaned forward, placing his hands on his knees as he started laughing. "You little wart, you're pulling my leg."

"No, I'm not shitting you; that's our names. Well, it ain't our real names; it's our nicknames. We all have nicknames. What is your name?"

"My name is Felix Ketterman. This is my barn."

"Your barn? I didn't think it belonged to anybody. It's setting out here all by itself, and there ain't nothing in it, except this basketball."

"Have you been out here before?"

"No. This is the first time. I was out for a walk this morning. And I've been looking at this big barn sticking up on this hill all by itself. Hell, you can see it from clear down there at the crossroads. I'm sort of curious about things anyway. So I just had to come take a look. I hope you don't care."

"I don't care. How old are you, Fuzzy?"

"I'm 12. How old are you?"

"I'm 79. How about a game of horse?"

Fuzzy tilted her head to the side a little and got a sly grin on her lips.

"You want to play me in a game of horse?"

"Yes. Let's you and I have a game."

"You're telling me an old man like you can still shoot a basketball?"

He never answered. He took the ball from Fuzzy and shot a one-hand set shot. The ball swished the net. "What do you think of that?"

"Well, I'll just be damned. You can shoot."

"You're pretty free with the cuss words for a young lady."

"Yeah, but I don't use the name of the Lord in any of them. And I know I should start stopping. I don't use very many. Mostly I just say shit and damn and hell, but I've been cussing ever since I learned how to talk, so it just comes natural for me."

"Yes, you really should start stopping, as you put it."

"I'll try. Okay, let's get this game on."

Fuzzy and Old Man Ketterman played four games of horse. He let her win two of them, but he did it in a way that she thought she had really beaten him. Truthfully, nobody could come close to beating him; he was a crack shot."

Fuzzy said, "This has been fun. Do you care if I bring the boys out here?"

"No, I would enjoy having you and 'your' boys come out. However, I do want to know when you are here. So I want your promise you will always tell me when you are in the barn."

"I promise. Now I have to get home. Grandpa Frank might wonder where I am. He'll probably think I went over to see Flash, but if he calls over there and finds out I ain't there, he might get worried. And I don't want to worry him, because he really is a nice old fart. I don't know what I would have done if he hadn't picked me up that night."

Mr. Ketterman was thinking, "I don't know half of what that little girl is saying. She talks too fast for my old ears to keep up."

Frank had begun to wonder where Fuzzy was when he looked out and saw her coming toward the house. He went ahead and started fixing them some breakfast as Fuzzy came bubbling in the door.

"Oh, Grandpa, I just got back from Old Man Ketterman's barn. And I met him while I was there. Say, you ought to see him shoot the basketball. I mean, that old fart is good. And he told me I could bring my boys out there, only he wants us to tell him when we are there. And he told me I should start stopping on my cussing."

"Well, honey babe, he is right about your cussing. I guess it is a little difficult for you to stop when you're living with an old man who is also trying to watch his language."

"But you are doing a lot better. I ain't heard you say a real bad word for a long time. How come you call me honey babe sometimes?"

"Oh, that is just a love name I use when I think about you. I once had a very good friend I called honey babe."

"Was it a girl?"

"Yes, it was a girl. But things didn't work between us."

"But things are working out with us, ain't they?"

Frank held his arms out and said, "Come here. Things are working out great with us. You are, without a doubt, the best thing that has ever happened to me. I am still learning how to be a grandpa, but things are working out. They are working out real good."

"What are we having for breakfast, Grandpa Frank?"

An hour later, Bugs was calling to order their regular meeting at Couch's shelter house. "Okay, what have we got on tap for today?"

Fuzzy spoke up. "Old Man Ketterman's barn; that's what we got on tap."

"You mean that big old barn about a mile north, the one that sits up on the hill?"

"Yeah, Bugs. That's the one. I was out there this morning, and he's got a basketball shooting goal up in the hayloft,"

Foxtail said, "Oh, you was not. You wouldn't walk all the way out there all by yourself, just to check out an old barn."

Flash responded, "Huh, you don't know her like I do. She'd walk 10 miles by herself to check out something she was curious about." He continued. "Now, what about this barn?"

"Oh, guys, you have to go see it. It has a great big hayloft, and he has a basketball goal up there. It's in the middle of one side, and shooting baskets there is better than that outside one at school. If you miss up there, you don't have to run across the school yard to get the ball. It stays up there in the loft, unless it rolls down one of those climbing up holes."

"You have been out there this morning?"

"Yeah, Flash. I was out there. And I played four games of horse with Mr. Ketterman; he won two and I won two. I asked if I could bring you guys out there, and he said I could. Only he wants to know any time we are there, so we have to tell him; I promised."

Bugs stood up and said, "Let's go out there right now. We ain't got nothing better to do."

"Follow me, guys. I know the way better than any of you, because

I am experienced at getting out there."

They started walking with Fuzzy leading the pack. Knuckles speculated, "Why is it that us five boys let that little runt of a fuzzy-headed girl lead us around like we was bulls with rings in our noses?"

"I don't know," Foxtail added. "Let's take her down and tickle her until she pees her pants."

"You'll have to catch me first." She took off running like a deer with the hair flying in the wind. The boys all started running after her.

Ten minutes later Fuzzy and her boys were sitting on Mr. Ketterman's front porch, breathing heavily and trying to regain their breath.

From the door they heard, "Well, Miss Fuzzy. I take it these are 'your boys.'"

"Yep, here they are."

He stepped out on the porch.

Between heavy puffing breaths, she said, "Guys, this is Mr. Ketterman." She took a deep breath and exhaled. "You tell him who you are."

Bugs was the first to step forward and extend his hand. "I'm Bugs."

The rest of the boys followed and shook Mr. Ketterman's hand as they introduced themselves.

"It is nice to meet all you boys. And I must say I am impressed by the way each of you introduced yourself and shook my hand."

"Flash's Grandpa Tivitts taught all of them how to do that. He taught them that they should look a person straight in the eye and give them a firm hand shake, not a bone crusher, just a firm grip," Fuzzy explained.

"That was wise counsel. Now, I suppose you guys want to go try my basketball court?"

"Yeah, Fuzzy said she was out there this morning."

"And she said you was a pretty good shot."

"Is that all she said?"

"Well, she added — for an old fart."

Fuzzy whacked Knuckles on the shoulder for that remark.

When they reached the barn door, Mr. Ketterman stopped.

"Before we go in, I want to tell all of you something. There is one room in this barn that is off limits. You may play in the loft; you may crawl around and over the mangers; you may go into the open granaries, but that middle granary is for me only. Okay?"

Fuzzy was thinking, "Now why in the hell did he have to say that? Now if I can just keep from busting a gut to get in there and see what he has hid? Oh, boy, why did that old fart tell us about that granary?"

They all climbed up in the loft and had a great session of basketball. They played three on three, and Mr. Ketterman was the referee. The kids had a good time, and the old man thoroughly enjoyed their company. He even showed them what he called his five point star offense. The boys really liked learning all they could about basketball, because a year from now, they would be going to school at Owappaho, and they play basketball.

Once, while they were playing, the ball bounced across the loft floor and down the ladder hole. Fuzzy said, "I'll go get it."

Down the ladder she scurried. She picked up the ball where it stopped rolling. She looked up to see a heavy door latch on the middle door. She thought, "I guess that is Mr. Ketterman's secret room." She cupped her hands over her eyes and tried to peek through the crack around the door and through a small knothole, but all she could see was blackness.

From the loft she heard, "Hurry up, Fuzzy. What's taking you so long?"

She hurried back to the opening and tossed the ball up to Foxtail.

The following morning, Fuzzy was up early, as usual. But this time she had something else on her mind. She could not forget about the secret room in that old barn.

She said to herself, "It's a damn good thing I'm not a cat. I remember my grandma back in South Carolina used to tell me, when I was a little bitty girl, that my curiosity was going to get me in trouble. Then she would say, 'Curiosity killed the cat.' "

Fuzzy could hear Frank snoring. She checked the clock; it was only five-fifteen. She mumbled in a low tone, "Hell, he won't be awake for at least an hour. I'm going out there and check that secret room out."

Half an hour later, Fuzzy was in the barn and was trying to find a way to see into that middle granary. She went into the granary to the left of it, closed the door and tried to find a crack she could see through. There was none. Then she went to the granary on the other side; no luck there either.

Finally, she went back to the strange-looking door latch to try figuring it out again. She wiggled it and shook it, but she could not get it to open. Finally, she just leaned back against the manger, mumbling to herself, "That's the strangest-looking latch I have ever seen. It don't even have a keyhole one it."

Suddenly she heard a voice. "You won't be able to figure it out either."

Fuzzy jumped like she was shot, "Oh, shit, now I'm in trouble."

Mr. Ketterman stepped into the walkway. "You should be in trouble, you little snipe. I told you that room is off limits."

"I know you did, Mr. Ketterman; I'm sorry. Guess my grandma was right. She told me my curiosity was going to get me in trouble. Are you going to whip my ass?"

"No, I have no intentions of whipping you. Are you alone?"

"Yes, sir, I'm alone. But I'll get out of here, and I'll never do this again."

He held up a hand. "Just wait a minute. Let me think a little."

After a moment that seemed like an hour to Fuzzy, he continued. "I am going to show you what is in that granary, but you promise not to tell about what you see."

"Okay, I promise."

He then instructed Fuzzy, "Lift up that round handle. While it is up, pull it toward you and lift again."

The door came open, and Fuzzy said, "Well, I'll just be damned. That is the simplest complicated latch I ever seen."

Mr. Ketterman stepped into the granary, struck a match and put the match to the wick of a coal oil lamp. As he replaced the lamp globe, everything in the room was illuminated.

Fuzzy turned slowly as she looked all around. "Oh, my, Mr. Ketterman, this room is like a room in a house almost."

"I lived in this room for nearly a year, while I was waiting to move a house out here from Camp 4."

He continued, "Open the doors on that wardrobe cabinet."

Inside the cabinet, there was a long fancy wedding dress on one hanger and an Army uniform on a different hanger.

"Is that your wife's wedding dress?"

"Yes. It is getting almost yellow now, but she was very pretty, and it was snowy white in 1915."

"I suppose that is your Army uniform?"

"Yes, it is. As a matter of fact, we were married in those two garments."

Mr. Ketterman seated himself on a chair and told Fuzzy, "Go ahead. Look around. You may open the boxes if you wish."

He sat and watched as Fuzzy looked over the many dishes and other things of interest.

When she was inspecting the lace on the wedding dress, Mr. Ketterman asked, "Would you like to try it on?"

"Oh, Mr. Ketterman, you would let me do that?"

"Yes, I would. Now let's see if we can figure out how to get it on you."

He rose to his feet and took the wedding dress off the hanger.

Fuzzy said, "I never have wore a dress very much. I don't know how to start putting one like this on."

Mr. Ketterman instructed Fuzzy to extend her arms upward while he slipped the dress over her head and helped her put her arms in the long sleeves.

"Now, turn around and let me button it up." He fastened the buttons.

Fuzzy was looking at the ruffles on the sleeves when she remarked, "Your wife sure wasn't very big, was she?"

"She was four feet ten inches tall, and she never weighed a hundred pounds in her entire lifetime."

He removed a paper covering from the full-length mirror attached to one side of the wardrobe.

"Now, come here and look at yourself."

The dress was loose around her chest, and the hem was on the floor, but in the lamplight of that granary, Fuzzy's curly dark red hair and her dark brown eyes made a stunning image in that old mirror.

Fuzzy could not help but be mesmerized by her own image. She had never even seen herself in dress. Now she was looking at an image in a beautiful, long-sleeved, high-necked wedding dress. She slowly moved her head back and forth as she said, "Gosh, Mr. Ketterman, a fancy dress sure does make me look different, don't it?"

"Honey, there is only one other time in my life that I ever saw anyone as beautiful as you are right now."

"Is that when your wife had this on?"

"That's the time. Now, let's take it off so you can get on back home."

He carefully unbuttoned the dress, and Fuzzy stepped out of it. Mr. Ketterman was getting ready to put the dress back on the hanger when

Fuzzy came to him and hugged him.

"You're a nice man, Mr. Ketterman. I won't tell anyone, not even Flash, that you let me see your secret room."

Then she reached up, took Mr. Ketterman's wrinkled face in her hands, kissed him right on the mouth and took off for home.

As he watched her disappear out the door, he said aloud, "Frank, old friend, you are one very fortunate old fart."

Tater Diggin'

It was a warm early morning in late July when Flash was awakened by his grandmother and told he was wanted on the phone. He rubbed his eyes and shook his head, trying to get the sleepy cobwebs out of his brain as he made his way to the telephone and answered with a less than enthusiastic, " 'Lo, this is Flash."

A very excited Fuzzy on the other end responded, "Oh, Flash, you got to get over to Mrs. Skinnyflint's as quick as you can!"

"Why? What's going on over there?"

"I don't know what it is. But the strangest thing is happening. There are little white things all over one end of her garden.

"What do you mean, little white things?"

"I don't know exactly what they are, but there are lots of them."

"Where'd you say you was?"

"I ain't there right now, but those little white things are over at Mrs. Skinnyflints."

"You better quit calling her that. One of these days you're going to slip and say it to her face, and you'll be embarrassed. Her name is Schimmelfeinig."

"Whatever. The point is, are you coming?"

"Don't I usually come if you need something?"

"You call Bugs and have him call Knuckles and — oh, hell, you know about the telephone set-up."

"Wait a minute. Now tell me again. What am I supposed to tell them?"

"I'll talk real slow this time. There are a bunch of little white things rolling around in Mrs. Skinnyflint's garden. They are all sizes, from like a baseball down to a golf ball."

Now Flash is wide awake and getting curious about these strange little white things.

"You say they're white? Are you sure they ain't mushrooms?"

"I know for sure they ain't mushrooms. Hurry, they might get away before we can catch all of them."

Flash forgot all about breakfast. He called Bugs to deliver the message.

Bugs speculated, "Maybe they're albino moles. That's the only thing I can think they could be."

"Hurry up and get the other guys called. I'm heading over there right now."

Fifteen minutes later Fuzzy had all the boys assembled in front of Mrs. Schimmelfeinig's house."

"Okay, guys, let's be real quiet as we sneak around the house. We don't want to scare them all away."

So they all lined up behind Fuzzy and cautiously tiptoed around the house and out to the garden. When they arrived at the south end of the garden, all they could see was a potato fork sticking in the ground."

Fuzzy sneaked up to the potato fork and pushed it into the ground and turned up a hill of white potatoes. Their sizes varied from about that of a baseball to down to a golf ball. She shook the fork and the white potatoes fell on the ground, rolling off the hill.

"See. What'd I tell you? There they are."

The boys all stood motionless for a moment before the comments started.

"You little turd, you tricked us."

"Okay, what is she paying you for digging her taters?"

"Boy, have we ever been suckers!"

"Fuzzy, we ought to take you down right now and blister your butt."

Flash was silent as the other boys made their comments. All of them turned on their heels and walked away, mumbling as they headed back to their homes.

Finally Flash said, "I just don't know what to say. I don't know whether to laugh or bawl. You got me up from a sound sleep; got me all excited about 'these mysterious little white things'; had me calling all the other guys, and now I find out all you wanted was help digging taters."

"Are you mad at me, Flash?"

"You damn right I'm mad at you. You know I'll do anything for you. If you wanted help digging taters, why didn't you ask me to help you dig taters?"

"I'm sorry. I just thought it would be a fun way to get everybody together."

"How much is she paying you?"

"A dollar. I thought that would be enough for all of us to walk over to Owappaho and get a banana split. I wouldn't have took all of us long to dig the taters."

"What would you have done if it had been me calling you with a big lie?"

"You're still mad, ain't you?"

He stood looking down at her tiny frame for a full minute before, without another word, he slowly turned and started walking away. He didn't take more than three steps when he heard Fuzzy start crying. He stopped and turned abruptly, "That fake crying ain't going to do you —"

Fuzzy had picked up the fork and started digging. Her back was to Flash, and he could see her shake as she really was trying to control her sobs. He couldn't take seeing her cry.

"Okay, Fuzzy, I'll help you dig taters."

She wiped her eyes on her sleeve. "I really am sorry, Flash. I don't ever want you to get mad at me. It was a dirty trick, and I really am sorry."

He reached out and put his hand on her shoulder, "It's okay. I ain't mad any more."

She threw both arms around his neck, gave him a long hug and held on to him tightly. Flash hesitated a short moment, but then put both arms around her and hugged her up close.

As he held her, he said, "Well, squirt, I guess we had our first fight. But I sure like this making up."

He turned her loose and said, "Let's get to digging taters."

The Soapbox Derby

FLASH WAS AWAKENED by the sound of something pecking on his bedroom window. He looked at his clock and said right out loud, "Holy Karukus, it's only five-thirty." He heard, "Flash! Open your window and let me in; it's raining out here and I'm getting wet."

Flash got out of bed and went to the window. He barely had the window up six inches before a head poked in. A soaking wet Fuzzy slid through the opening and onto the bedroom floor.

Flash quickly closed the window. "Fuzzy, what are you doing out in the rain at five-thirty in the morning?"

"You got a towel? I'm wetter'n a drowned rat."

He hurried into the bathroom and grabbed a big bath towel. As he handed it to Fuzzy, he realized all he had on was his jockey shorts.

"Dad gum it, Fuzzy, here you are in my bedroom, and all I got on is my shorts."

He hurried over to get his overalls and shirt, as she answered, "Heck, it don't bother me none, I've seen Grandpa Frank in his shorts lots of times."

"Well, I ain't used to having a girl in my bedroom, especially when all I got on is my shorts."

"I've got something important to talk about. I've been awake since three-thirty and I couldn't wait any longer."

"First we have to get you warmed up; your teeth are chattering like a chipmunk and you're shivering all over."

She answered, "I'm getting dried off now, so I'll just jump in your bed and get in your warm spot before it cools off."

Flash started to say something, but she tossed the towel on the floor and crawled in bed and pulled the covers up to her chin, saying, "Oh, this feels good."

Flash grabbed his head as he thought, "She's going to get my bed wet; Grandma is going to think I peed the bed."

Then he said, "Well, my butt won't feel very good if Grandma comes in here right now. I don't think she would approve of me having a girl in my bed, even if it's you."

"Even if it's me? You mean she might not care too much if it was me?"

"Well, she knows I like you and she says you're a good kid."

"Oh, Flash, really? Then maybe she wouldn't care if you got in here with me and warmed me up more. I'm still shivering."

"You'll get warmed up soon enough. Now what is so important that you had to come over here so early?"

"Sit down over here on the bed and I'll tell you."

He sat down on the edge of the bed, and she started talking so fast he had to have her slow down and start over. She had seen a poster somewhere that told of all the events that would be taking place at the annual Owappaho homecoming celebration. Camp 4 is practically a suburb of Owappaho, and they have a parade and a carnival and a whole bunch of activities there every fall, and added to the activities this year would be a soapbox derby.

The Owappaho water tower is located right at the very top of a high hill, and Main Street goes right up to the water tower. The city council voted to let the WPA replace the old brick street with a new concrete street, and then someone had the idea of the soapbox derby, since the new street would be so suitable for something like this event.

Fuzzy said, "There will be three different age groups; eight- to 10-year-olds; 10- to 12-year-olds and 12- to 14-year-olds. And they are giving $25 for first place, $10 for second place and $5 for third place. I just know we can build a racer that could win something."

"Wow! Fuzzy, that is a great idea. And I think you are right. We not only can build a winner, we will BE a winner."

Without a warning, Fuzzy reached up and grabbed Flash by the ears, pulled his face down to hers and kissed him.

He jumped to his feet as she said, "Don't you dare wipe that off."

"I'm not wiping it off, I rubbing it in."

"Oh, you are not, you're wiping it off."

"You're warmed up now, you better get out of my bed before Grandma comes in here and sees you there."

"I think I'll just take all my clothes off under these covers."

"Don't you dare do that, you little fart."

"Okay." She threw the covers back and stood up. "Let's go into the kitchen table and make some plans. You got some paper and pencils?"

"Yeah, I have paper and pencil."

They tiptoed quietly past his grandparents' bedroom door; they were both snoring.

Fuzzy remarked, "Huh, you didn't have to worry about Grandma catching me in your bed. I'll bet a freight train going down the hall wouldn't wake them up."

When they reached the kitchen, Flash turned on the light and asked, "Would you like a glass of juice or some milk?"

"I'd rather have a cup of coffee."

"Do you still drink coffee?"

" 'Course I do; I like it."

"No wonder you're such a runt; coffee stunts your growth, you know."

"That's okay, I don't want to get very big anyway. But I guess I would take a glass of milk and some cookies, if you have them."

"We got some oatmeal cookies. Is that okay?"

While he was getting the milk and cookies, Fuzzy started telling about how her Grandpa Frank used to be a big-time collector of Indian relics, and that he had a big tin arrowhead that might be used for a body.

"We could split it right down the middle and make the body of a race car out of half of it."

Flash asked, "Do you think he might get a little upset if we used his arrowhead?"

"Nah, if I ask him for it real nice, I know he would give me anything he had. He never gets pissed off at me."

"You shouldn't say 'pissed off,' Fuzzy, it ain't lady like."

"Pissed off ain't using the name of the Lord in vain."

"It still ain't very lady like."

"Okay, I won't do it anymore."

"Now, what about this arrowhead thing?"

"It's about four feet long and 30 inches wide and 10 inches thick. It is hollow, and the tin is only about as thick as heavy paper; I already measured it. And if we split it from the front tip to the back with tin snips, we can have a half of an arrowhead that is 15 inches high, 10 inches wide and four feet long. Then if we have a wreck while we're testing our racer, we will have a spare body."

"Ten inches ain't very wide, and 15 inches high ain't big enough for a guy to get inside of."

"I know it ain't big enough for a guy, but I can fit in it. We'll be a racing team, and I can be the driver."

"Well, we will have to have a meeting with Bugs, Squarehead, Foxtail and Knuckles before we make any important decisions like who the driver will be."

"That's fine, but look here at this drawing. See, we can take a one 1x12 board that is four feet long, put the arrowhead half on the board and trace around the edge. Then we can use Grandpa Frank's bandsaw to cut out the frame part. Then we can fasten the sides to the 1x4 with nails and attach the two axles with wheels. The front axle can be on a center pivot, and the driver can sit up and guide the racer with little ropes, just like you're driving a team of horses."

"You know something, Fuzzy, I like this idea. Then we can cut a little slit in the front where the driver can look out and see."

"Yes, and we can cut a hole in one side big enough for me to squeeze in, save the piece we cut out, and then fasten it back on with hinges and a closer catch."

While they were making plans, Grandpa came shuffling into the kitchen and turned on the coffeepot. He hardly noticed the kids as he shuffled back into his bedroom.

Fuzzy's reaction was, "Hot dog, the coffee pot is going. I need a cup of coffee to get going in the mornings."

"How much coffee do you drink?"

"Just one cup a day — most of the time — sometimes I drink two or three — or four."

"By the way, Fuzzy, let's not say too much about your arrowhead design until we know for sure what the rest of the gang wants to do. We might want to enter more than one racer in this race. In fact, I think we should suggest we break up in pairs and build three racers. We could win first, second and third that way. Wow, that would be $40."

"Yeah, we could do a lot with that kind of money. And besides, we can have a little friendly competition."

Fuzzy was drinking coffee, and Flash was looking at her drawings when his grandpa walked back into the kitchen. He was tousle-headed and sleepy-eyed as he went for the coffee pot, poured himself a cup of coffee and sat down at the table with Fuzzy and Flash. He yawned and stretched, and then he said, "Morning, kids." Then it dawned on him that Fuzzy was not usually sitting at the breakfast table at six-thirty in the morning.

"Well, well — ah, Fuzzy! What are you doing here so early in the morning?"

"Oh, Flash and I had some important business to talk over."

"You're making wedding plans?"

"Now, Grandpa! Don't you start that!"

"You mean you're already married?"

Fuzzy started giggling, and Grandpa reached over and ruffled up her hair. "You little rascal, I always was partial to redheads."

"They ain't no doubt about my hair being red, is there?"

"Are you going to stay and have breakfast with us?"

"Flash and I have already had a couple of oatmeal cookies and a big glass of milk, and I'm having a cup of coffee."

"When did you start drinking coffee?"

"Oh, I started drinking coffee when I was still living with my grandma back in South Carolina, when I was just a little kid."

Flash added, "You ain't much bigger'n a little kid now, and if you keep on drinking coffee, you might not get any bigger."

"Oh, poof. Let's talk about our plan."

"What's this drawing here on the table? It looks like half of an arrowhead."

"It is half of an arrowhead. It's the design of a soapbox racer me'n Flash are going to build. Then we're going to enter it in the race over at Owappaho."

"What are you going to use for wheels?"

"Grandpa, we don't have the wheels and axles yet; we have to find them."

"Guess what? I just happen to remember that your Grandpa Frank has a set of those real narrow hard rubber-tired wheels, like were used on the original soapbox racers. He bought them at auction sale one day; I was there."

"Wow! Do you think he might let us use them?"

"As a matter of fact, he also has the axles — including the pivot mechanism for the front axle. And I'll just bet he will let you have all of that stuff."

Fuzzy jumped to her feet. "He'll let me have anything I want. And I'll bet he'll help us build it in his shop."

She started dancing around and yelling, "Whoopee!"

Suddenly she stopped dancing and bent over. "Oh my, I got so excited, I peed a little bit." She headed for the bathroom.

Grandpa laughed so hard he started coughing, and his eyes started watering. He was so tickled he almost passed out for a little bit. Grandma heard all the laughing and coughing, so she got up and came out in the kitchen.

"What's so funny? And why are you two up so early?"

"Oh, Grandpa is laughing 'cause Fuzzy peed her pants and had to make a quick run for the bathroom."

"Fuzzy peed her pants *(pause)*. Fuzzy peed her pants? What is

Fuzzy doing here? Am I being held in the dark for some reason?"

Grandpa got more tickled at that. He tried to tell Granny why he was laughing so hard, but he couldn't even talk; he just got worse. Somewhere in his laughing, he managed to say that Fuzzy and Flash were making plans for the wedding. So that called for an explanation about the soapbox derby.

Grandma started back toward the bedroom, but she suddenly whirled around and asked, "What wedding?"

Grandpa started laughing harder.

Grandma put her hands on her hips and said, "Just what in the hell is going on here this morning?"

Fuzzy had come out of the bathroom and was standing behind Grandma.

"I have to go home and get some different jeans. I peed more than I thought I did."

Grandma turned around and looked at Fuzzy. "Marvelle, you are all wet. Did you pee your pants?"

Fuzzy held her hands out, elbows at her sides, palms up, and said, "No, I just got back from a swim in razor pit?"

Grandpa lost it again. He left the room saying, between coughs, tears and gasping, "Oh, this is the best laugh I've had since my wedding night."

Grandma grabbed a loaf of bread from the counter and threw it at him. She hit him in back of the head, and bread slices flew all over the hall. She went back to bed; Grandpa went to the bathroom: Fuzzy went home, and Flash got stuck picking up the bread slices.

The rain stopped falling a little after noon, so Flash called Bugs, and he called a meeting at his house at two o'clock that afternoon. Everybody showed up on time except Knuckles, but he wasn't very late. When Flash got there, Fuzzy pulled him aside and whispered in his ear, "If you promise not to tell them about me peeing my pants, I promise I won't tell them I was in your bed at five-thirty this morning."

Flash whispered, "You blackmailing little fart. Of course, I won't tell anything; you know that."

They talked about the soapbox race, and everyone was in favor of entering. Flash suggested they might even want to consider breaking up in pairs and having a friendly competition of their own with three racers.

Everybody seemed to like the idea of entering three racers, so Bugs said, "All in favor of three cars, raise their right hand."

The vote was unanimous. Bugs then added, "Since I am the chairman of the committee, I will appoint the pairs. Fuzzy, you and Flash are sweet on each other anyway, so you two will be one pair."

Flash winked at Fuzzy, and she gave him a big smile.

"Knuckles and Squarehead will be the second team, and Foxtail and I will make up the third team. Are there any objections? *(pause)* There being no objections, it is so ordered. Let's get started."

Fuzzy had a question. "What about the numbers we paint on our cars?"

"Good point, Fuzzy. But I know how to solve it. Flash, your birthday is in February and Fuzzy's is in March, so your car can be number 23. Knuckles was born in January and Squarehead was born in September, so you guys can number your car 19; Foxtail and I were both born in August, so our car will be number 88. How does that sound?"

"That sounds great, but what about colors?"

They decided to write red, green, blue, yellow, orange, purple, black and white on separate pieces of paper, fold them up tightly and put them in a box. Then they drew for a color. Fuzzy drew for her team, and she unfolded yellow. Bugs drew Red and Foxtail drew white. They decided to use colors of their own choice for wheels, trim and numbers.

They also agreed not spy on each other or try to copy any designs. They would keep their team cars a secret, right up to the day of the races. They would still have the usual weekly meetings, but talk about the secret racers would be forbidden.

One day while Bugs and Foxtail were trying to decide on a design for their racer, Bugs said. "You know something, Foxtail. I have been thinking; one of the main things about building a race car like this is how much wind resistance will hold it back. The skinnier it is, the better it will slice through the air. The front end needs to be almost sharp, like a knife blade."

"I think I know what you're getting at, Bugs. The bigger the driver is, the wider and higher the car has to be. So, if the driver is a little skinny fart like Fuzzy, they have an advantage."

"You got it, Foxtail. And neither one of us is very skinny."

"You're right, Bugs. But what if we get Turnip to be our driver?"

"That is exactly what I am getting at. With her as our driver, we can build a car that is real skinny. You call her tonight and see if she is willing."

Bugs said, "My Uncle Charlie is metal worker. He builds those round hollow pipes they put in buildings to push air through from the furnace all over the building. Last week when he stopped by our house, I saw some scraps in his pickup. I asked him if I could have one of them. I wasn't even thinking about this car race, of course, but I have just what we need."

"What does it look like?"

"It is just the end that was cut off a great big metal pipe. It is about two feet tall and three feet across the middle. We can flatten it down and then pound the bended edges until we make it like a great big double-edge knife blade. Then we can spread it open just enough for Turnip to sit down in it and attach it to a board with wheels on it."

That evening, Foxtail called Turnip and told her about their plan. She was really excited about it. She said, "Maybe my dad will let us build it right here in our garage."

Foxtail said, "That would be great. We need a secret place to build it."

Then Turnip asked, "Do you already have the wheels?"

"No, we still have to get some."

"What about an old baby buggy, would that work?"

"Turnip, do you have an old baby buggy? That would be perfect."

"Yes, we have one that Dad has been threatening to throw in the junk."

So now Bugs and Foxtail had all they needed. They could not wait to see the faces on the others when they learned Turnip was the driver of number 88.

The buggy had immovable axles on the front and back, so Bugs and Foxtail fixed individual back wheel brakes, so Turnip could keep the racer from veering off the straight line by simply applying a little brake on one or the other of the rear wheels. It worked great as a steering device, but it did slow them up a bit. However, since the course of the race was straight down the hill, she had to steer very little.

Knuckles and Squarehead didn't actually build a car; they just removed the peddling mechanism from and old pedal car Knuckles had, lubricated the wheels, and Squarehead drove it in the race.

The kids all enjoyed the following three weeks with great anticipation. The racer Fuzzy and Flash made was a simple design, but that arrowhead made it as aerodynamic as anything could be. Frank Thomas let them use his shop and tools. He helped them as they got the flat board frame cut out perfectly. The half arrowhead fit on it just as planned, but before they put screws in to hold it in place, they had to secure the back axle and wheels. Then they added the front axle and wheels with its pivot in the center and tied ropes next to each front wheel. Fuzzy sat on the frame while Flash pushed her as fast as he could run. The rope steering set-up worked great. He tried it, too, but he realized he could not fit in the car when they got the body fastened.

After they had the frame finished, they fastened the body with screws, drilled two holes for the steering ropes on the front of the body and cut out a windshield slit about two inches wide and six inches long so Fuzzy could see to drive. A decision was made to make an entry hole near the back right side where Fuzzy could crawl through and sit in a bent-over position with her feet up in the front of the arrowhead. She had to be a contortionist to get in and out, but once she was in position, she could steer real good, and she was not uncomfortable either.

They painted the racer with two coats of bright yellow paint, painted the wheels black and put the number 23 on both sides. They were ready to roll. Grandpa Frank's garage was an excellent place to do the work, so he knew all about what was going on, and he was getting as excited about the race as the kids were.

Grandpa Tivitts came over one day and told them something that was to be a real significant factor in the project; he told them he had some light-weight grease that had graphite in it, and that graphite made any grease or oil slicker, so that's what they used to oil the wheels. He also told them to take some real fine sandpaper and sand the axles where the wheels fit on until they shined like a mirror, and to wrap some sandpaper around a dowel pin so they could shine up the inside of the wheel as well.

On completion of the racer, Grandma got the Kodak and took a picture of Fuzzy and Flash standing with the car in front of them. When she went back in the house, Flash turned to Fuzzy and said, "Fuzzy, this has been the funnest thing I have ever done. I want to win the race, and I think we will, but really the most fun was just building it with you."

She turned to him and said, "Why, you big old softie."

He grabbed her and give her the biggest hug he could.

"Don't squeeze me too tight; you want me to pee my pants again?"

He immediately turned her loose.

Saturday was the big event. They loaded the racer in the back of Grandpa Frank's pickup truck, covered it up with a sheet and headed for the Owappaho water tower. All the contestants were directed to be there by one o'clock for the position drawings. The race was scheduled for 2 p.m. There were nine cars in the 12- to 14-year-old age group, and the street was marked off with 10 lanes, so there would be only one heat in the 12-year-old division. Somebody had built a starting gate thing that had a hinged rod sticking up in front of each car. When it was time to start the race, the starter pulled a lever that lowered all the hinged rods at the same time, and the cars were off.

The hill was not exceptionally steep for the first 30 yards, so even if the cars started off without being pushed and movement was slow at the beginning, the hill soon began to become steeper. It didn't take long for gravity to have its effect. The main factors in the speed of the cars were wind resistance, how well the wheels were lubricated, and the amount of friction between axles and the wheels and the wheels and the road.

An arrowhead does not catch very much wind; graphite lubrication makes wheels roll easily, and tiny hard rubber tires do not cause much friction on the road. It was obvious to everyone, the yellow number 23 was going to win the race, because by the time Fuzzy reached the mid-point of the race, she had a good three-foot lead and was gaining more with every yard the racer rolled. The #23 car crossed the finish line 10 feet ahead of the second place car, #88.

With the race won, they now discovered they had forgotten an important component; the car didn't have brakes, and Fuzzy couldn't even get a foot on the ground to slow it down. She sped past the finish line and on down the hill. People were jumping out of the way, and she was weaving all over the street and yelling, "Get the hell out of the way, I ain't got no brakes on this damn thing."

Flash was running as fast as he could, trying to catch up. He was thinking, "I'll never know how she managed to miss all those people. It was just lucky there wasn't a baby in that stroller she knocked stem-winding."

When the car finally began to slow down, some big high school girl grabbed it and stopped it.

Fuzzy was still in the car when Flash caught up with her.

He asked, "Are you okay?"

"Hell, no, I'm not okay! Push me over to the courthouse bathrooms; I think I did a little more than pee my pants this time."

Flash told her they had won the $25.

"I know, I know, but I'm in no condition to get the prize right now. Push me to the bathroom, and hurry."

He pushed the car over to the courthouse and helped Fuzzy get out. She hurried inside, and he waited by the car. After a few minutes, she came back and said, "Well, I guess that was a false alarm; all I did was fart. But I was so scared I didn't know what to do. When that baby stroller went flying in the air, I thought I would faint. Why didn't you think about brakes? You're the guy. Guys are supposed to know stuff like that."

"I'm sorry I didn't think about brakes. But you are okay, and we did win first place."

"How did the other two cars do?"

"Bugs and Foxtail, with Turnip driving, were in second place. Squarehead and Knuckles got sixth place. Now we have to get the car back to collect our prize and have our picture taken for the paper."

The next day a picture of Fuzzy and Flash, standing by race car number 23, appeared on the front page of the *Owappaho Chief*. They even won trophies.

Flash told Fuzzy she could keep the first place trophy, because she had earned it. And Bugs and Foxtail thought Turnip should keep the second place trophy. They put the $35 in the gang savings account at the bank.

UFO

LAST NIGHT, AT the scout meeting, Bugs, Foxtail, Knuckles, Squarehead and Flash tried to talk their scoutmaster into taking all of them on an overnight fishing trip. But he told them he was sorry because he had already promised his wife to do something with her. Flash was really disappointed because the weather was perfect. The forecast called for mild temperatures, no wind and a clear moonlit night. You couldn't find a better August night for a fishing camp-out. But they knew if Mr. Frisbee said he couldn't make it, it wasn't because he didn't want to. So they didn't make much of a fuss about it. They just decided there would be another time later on.

The next day turned out to be a record-setting day. It was as warm as a summer day, and the weatherman said the temperature should not get lower than 60 degrees during the upcoming night. Bugs stopped Flash by his locker at school and said, "You know what I think, Flash? I think we should go ahead and have our own fishing camp-out. It don't need to be a scout thing."

"I think that's a great idea, Bugs. Lets see what the other guys think about it."

Then a voice behind him said, "What's a great idea? Don't you lunkheads go planning anything without letting me in on it."

Flash turned around to answer. "Well, Fuzzy, we are talking about an overnight camp-out and fishing trip. I don't think girls ought to be included in something like that."

"Hey, Flash, you know I can fish as good as any of you guys."

"Yes, I know you can fish as good as us, but I don't think Grandpa Frank would want you camping out all night with a bunch of boys."

"Oh, poof! He don't give a hoot what I'm doing. Once I go to my room at night, I never see him again until the next evening."

"Well, we ain't made any real plans yet anyway."

"Just don't make any definite plans without telling me about them."

Flash thought, "Oh, boy, how am I going to handle this? I really like Fuzzy, but an overnight fishing trip ain't no place for girls. But I can't lie to her."

The boys had physical education class the last period of the day, so they got a chance to talk about their plans as they were leaving class. They decided they would get their stuff together as soon as supper was over and meet out at the south bend of Turkey Creek. They wouldn't wear scout outfits, but they would take their backpacks. They knew their folks wouldn't mind if they had an all-night fishing camp out. But Flash also knew his grandma wouldn't approve of Fuzzy coming along.

They figured they would have just enough time to get out there, pitch the tents, start a campfire and set a few limb lines before it got dark. They were all getting excited about it, because they had not been on an overnight since August.

The telephone rang while Flash and his grandparents were eating supper. Grandpa answered it. "It's for you, Ernie."

"Who is it?"

"Now, who would you guess it is?"

Flash thought, "Oh, nuts, that little runt. Now what am I going do about her. I don't want to hurt her feelings"

He went in the other room and picked up the receiver. "Hi, Fuzzy, I was just about to call you."

"Yeah, right! I bet you were. What did you guys decide?"

"Now, Fuzzy, you know I like you, and I wouldn't do anything to hurt your feelings. But the truth is, there are some things that are reserved just for boys, just the same as there are some things reserved just for girls."

He was surprised by her answer.

"I know, Flash. You are right. If I went out on an overnight fishing trip with all you guys, some of my girlfriends would accuse me of being a slut."

"Oh, they wouldn't do that, would they?"

"Oh, yeah. I can just hear Margie Lampus say, "There is only one thing wrong with a fishing trip — some of the boys might actually want to fish."

"Then you understand, don't you?"

"I understand. I hope you guys have a good time and catch a bunch of fish."

"Fuzzy, if I was there where you are, I would grab you by the ears and give you a kiss this time."

"Well, it don't take long to get over here. But I won't hold my breath until you get here."

"Good night, Fuzzy."

"Good night, Flash."

Just as they had planned, they had enough time to walk out to Turkey Creek, build a campfire and set the limb-lines before it got dark. They decided they didn't need the tents. They would just use their backpacks for pillows and sit around the fire.

There was not a cloud in the sky, and the moon was so bright they could see the limbs they had lines tied on without using flashlights. The fish were not biting, so they just sat around the fire and enjoyed the unusually warm night. Squarehead and Knuckles soon went to sleep, and Foxtail was getting so sleepy he dropped out of the conversation.

Bugs and Flash were leaning back on their packs and looking up through the trees at the many stars when Flash noticed what appeared to be unusually bright lights on an approaching airplane. He said, "Look over there, Bugs. Did you ever see such bright lights on a plane?"

"Wow! They really are bright."

Then as they were both looking at the moving lights, a very bright spot began to appear at the front of the object. The bright spot kept getting bigger and bigger as it grew into an intensely bright light that resembled the flash of an electric welder. It was so bright they had to turn their eyes away.

At this point, Bugs and Flash shook the other guys who were sleeping, saying, "Hey, wake up, you guys. Look at that light."

They roused up as the intense light began to fade away. As it faded, the object they assumed to be a plane seemed to be stopped in mid-air. Then they could see what appeared to be sunlight reflecting off flat panels on top of the object as it slowly turned.

They were all on their feet and wide awake, and they could plainly see something moving in the sky, and it was headed directly to where they were camping. They stood transfixed and silent as they watched a huge object that was shaped something like a kite move slowly through the sky in their direction.

There was no sound coming from the object, but there were many lights on it. In the front, there were two big round glowing lights that resemble a round fluorescent light fixture. On each side there were two more of these big round lights, and in the center of the object there were four of the same lights arranged in a diamond configuration. From the rear light of the diamond formation to the back end of the thing, there were three more lights spaced at equal distances apart. One of these lights was green, one was red and the rear light was the same as all the other large lights. Throughout all the rest of the spaces between the lights were hundreds of tiny lights that resembled the lights of a city when you are looking down on it from high on a hill or up in an airplane.

None of the boys made a sound as they all stood and observed this "thing" move slowly over their heads. They could not figure out how big it was because it made no sound in the quiet night. All they could do is stand, wide-mouthed and open-eyed, and watch it creep across the sky directly over their heads. They watched it until it seemed to be well past their position, and then, poof! It was suddenly gone. It just disappeared without leaving a trace of a smoke or vapor trail of any kind.

The boys stood silently for several moments before they began to discuss what they had seen. Flash said, "I think it was about 500 feet above us, and it was about as big as a football field."

Bugs added, "I think it was much bigger. I think it was maybe 30,000 feet in the air, and it was as big as a good-sized city."

Knuckles added, "If it was as high as you think, Bugs, then it was not traveling real fast, but if it was as high as Flash thinks, it was really moving slow."

"Yeah, from the ground, an airliner traveling at 500 miles an hour looks like it is moving slow."

"And how come there was no sound coming from it?"

"I wonder if those big round lights were actually the engines. Or maybe they were some kind of anti-gravity engine?"

"We know for sure it wasn't a flying saucer, because it was not round. It was shaped more like a great big kite, wasn't it?"

"Yeah, it was shaped like a kite. And that sucker was real big."

"It wasn't big; it was huge."

"It was awesome."

Bugs looked at his watch. "It ain't very late. It's only nine-fifteen."

Flash added, "I think we better get our things together and get back to town. I wonder if anyone else saw it."

Everybody must have agreed with Flash, because without another word, they gathered their stuff up and headed home.

Flash rushed into the house to tell his grandparents what they had seen. They were both asleep, so he picked up the phone and called Fuzzy.

She answered, "Oh, Flash, you are not going believe what I saw awhile ago. Just as you called, I was making a drawing of it and writing it down just as I remembered it."

"Oh, yes, I am gonna believe it; I think we all saw the same thing. It went right over above where we were camping."

"Okay, tell me what you saw."

So Flash described what he had seen to her. The only difference in their stories came when he told about seeing what they thought was an airplane and then seeing it come to a stop with that bright light.

Fuzzy said, "That bright light is what caught my attention. I was in bed looking toward my bedroom window when all at once the sky just lit up like someone turned on a bright light. I got up and went to the window. That's when I saw it moving slowly across the sky."

"If we saw it, then there must have been a lot of other people who saw it, too. Did you tell your Frank?"

"I never even thought about telling him. I just sat down and started drawing a picture of what I saw. Then I wrote out a story about it, just like I saw it."

"That was a great idea, Fuzzy. I think I am going call all the other guys and tell them to draw a picture of what we saw and write a story about it before we forget anything. I tell you what. Will you call Knuckles and Foxtail? I'll call Bugs and Squarehead and Mr. Timms. Since he is our teacher when school starts, he might have some more ideas about what we should do."

"Okay, then why don't we all meet somewhere later so we can compare our stories?"

"I'll call Mr. Timms first and see what he thinks we should do."

Flash called Mr. Timms and told him the whole story. He advised them, "Call everybody back and tell them to make the drawings and write the stories. Then tomorrow morning, all of you meet me at the school where we will compare how each of you remember what you saw."

They all did as Mr. Timms suggested.

He sat down and read all of the stories and looked at all of the drawings. Then he pinned all our drawings up on the bulletin board, side by side.

We all looked at those drawings. Then we looked around at each other. Then we looked back at the drawings.

Squarehead was the first to speak up. "From the looks of them drawings, I can't believe we all seen the same thing."

Then we started talking about our drawings. We all agreed that my drawing and Fuzzy's drawing looked more alike than any of the others, but we couldn't agree that they looked more like what we had seen.

"Okay, people," Mr. Timms said. "Everybody have a seat while I read the stories you have written."

It took almost an hour for him to cipher out what all of us had written, but he finally did. When he was finished, he said, "Okay, now I am going to take what I have gleaned from all your stories and from your drawings and draw the UFO on the blackboard as I interpret your ideas.

He picked up a box of colored chalk and started drawing on the board. Before he was half done, we all agreed that what he was drawing looked more like what we had seen than any of our own drawings did.

Mr. Timms looked around the room at all of us for a moment. "Does this experience tell you people anything?"

We didn't know how to answer his question.

He continued. "Isn't it strange how the human mind works? I do not doubt for one second that all of you saw this 'thing' in the sky last night. You are all bright young people and you all have good vision. Yet, look how differently you interpreted what you saw."

"Mr. Timms …"

"Yes, Foxtail, what do you have to say?"

"Do you reckon anyone else seen that big thing in the sky last night?"

"I guess we will know before long. If it was seen by others, surely it will be reported."

They all watched the TV news, checked the papers and listened to the radio. Nothing further was ever said. But they all knew that thing was there. They were wide awake and they were all alert. They could not have been imagining things. Yet, they all saw something different in the same thing.

Flash said, "I know the others feel much the same as I do. That evening put an entire different perspective on our way of thinking. We have quit making fun of UFO stories and have begun to realize that, as we stare up into the millions of little twinkling stars at night, there is little doubt in our minds that we are not the only planet in the heavens with life on board."

Fuzzy Has a Fight

FLASH AND GRANDPA were sitting in the porch swing one late afternoon, when they looked down the road toward Owappaho and saw Fuzzy coming their way.

Flash remarked, "Look at that! Here comes Fuzzy. She told me she was tired and was going home to rest, and there she comes from Owappaho."

They watched her for a moment before they both noticed she was limping slightly.

Flash said, "I'll bet she has sprained that ankle again; I'd better go help her."

He stood up and started trotting toward Fuzzy. As he got closer, he could tell she was not only limping; she had a black eye, her shirt sleeve was torn, and she was holding her left wrist with her right hand.

"Fuzzy! What happened to you?"

"I've been in a fight."

"It looks like you got the bad end of it."

"Huh! You ought to see Margie Lumpus. I dumped a whole barrel of whoopass on her."

"Margie Lumpus! Fuzzy, she is as tall as me, and she weighs twice what you do."

"You ever hear the slogan, 'It ain't the size of the dog in the fight, it's the size of the fight in the dog'?"

"What was you fighting about?"

"Yesterday that heifer told me Grandpa Frank was a morphodite, and she also said he was a queer and a fag. She don't really know how to cuss, so she just calls people weird names. I didn't know what any of them things meant, so last night I asked Grandpa Frank. He told me they were not very nice words, and he wanted to know where I heard about them. I told him Margie was saying them, but I didn't tell him she was calling him that."

When Fuzzy and Flash reached the porch, Grandpa asked her what happened, and she told him the same things she had told Flash.

Grandpa speculated, "And then you went to town to confront her, didn't you?"

"I didn't confront her; I beat the crap out of her. That's why I'm holding my wrist. I punched her so many times, my wrist is almost broke, I think."

Grandpa turned to Flash. "Ernie, isn't that Lumpus girl that big girl that played baseball with the Pirates?"

"That's the one, Grandpa."

"And you say you beat the crap out of her?" He was restraining his laughter.

"I put her down the road, bawling like a calf looking for its mother."

Grandma had joined the scene and heard the discussion. "Come on in the house and let me doctor those scrapes and scratches."

Fuzzy continued, "She didn't only call Grandpa Frank nasty names, she said I was a lesserbean, or something like that. I don't know what that is either, but I figured if those other words were bad, so was a lesserbean."

Flash asked, "What do those words mean, Grandpa?"

He answered, "As soon as Grandma gets Fuzzy doctored up, we will sit down and I will explain them to you."

Ten minutes later, Fuzzy, Flash and Grandpa were sitting on the porch, and Grandpa began to explain the new terms to the kids.

"In the first place, the first word is not 'morphodite'; it is hermaphrodite. And rest assured, Grandpa Frank is not one. It means that sometimes, very rarely, a creature will be born that is both male and female. In some lower animals, it occurs more often. However, in very rare instances, it does occur in people."

Fuzzy asked, "What do they do about it?"

"Well, Fuzzy, actually, I don't really know what they do about it. I have never heard of anyone like that. Like I say, it is very rare."

"But, for sure, Grandpa Frank ain't that?" she asked.

"Positively not," Grandpa replied.

Grandpa continued, "Now, as for the other words: queer and fag and 'lesserbean.' The word is 'lesbian," not lesserbean, and it means — let's see, how will I put this? It means a woman who really wants to be a man, or who actually believes she is a man. She does not want to date or marry a man; she wants to marry a woman."

Flash piped up, "Well, that sure ain't Fuzzy. I know for sure."

Fuzzy added, "I sure wouldn't be kissing on you if I was, would I?"

Grandpa quizzed, "Oh! So you've been kissing on Flash, have you?"

"What about those other words?" Flash quickly asked.

Fuzzy added, "Yeah, what about 'queer' and 'fag'?"

"Those two words are slang words that refer to someone who is homosexual."

Fuzzy asked, "Homosexual, what's a homosexual?"

"That is a man who really wants to be a woman, a man who thinks he is a woman. I don't understand all about this subject, but men who are like that are called homosexuals, and women are called lesbians. The crude words for those conditions are fag and queer, and I think there are others, but they don't come to mind."

The two youngsters sat for a moment, digesting what they had heard.

Then Fuzzy asked, "What causes it, Grandpa?"

"I really don't know what causes it. It is a subject that is just not discussed very much. I have heard that some experts are convinced people are born that way and can't help it. Others are convinced it is caused by the way a young child is raised."

After a pause, Flash said, "Boy, that's a terrible thing to happen to someone. Looks to me like they would get all confused and not know what they were."

"It would seem that way to me, Ernie, but like I say, it does not happen very often. However, there are a lot more homosexuals than there are hermaphrodites."

Fuzzy said, "You know something, Grandpa? If I was one of them homosexuals, I would just keep it to myself and not tell anyone about it."

"Actually, I have a feeling there are more of them than we know about, because of just what you said."

"Do you think Grandpa Frank might be, and just ain't saying anything about it?"

"No, Fuzzy. I know how much Frank wanted to get married at one time. He really did love that lady, and I think she loved him, but … well, things happen. But I can guarantee you that your Grandpa Frank is normal."

"I knew he was all the time, but just between you and Flash and me, I'm kind of glad Margie called Grandpa Frank those things. I have been looking for a good chance to whip her ass ever since she called me a slut, 'cause I run around with my boys."

Grandpa chuckled a bit and then added, "Seriously, kids, what we have been discussing is really tragic, in my opinion. I want you to know what those words mean, but I want you to promise me you will never call anyone by them."

Flash answered, "I won't, Grandpa."

Fuzzy added, "I won't either. But I can't say I won't call that Margie Lumpus a bitch, 'cause that is exactly what she is."

"Now, Fuzzy, I think you have already made your point with Margie. You don't need to agitate her. If she leaves you alone, then you leave her alone. Who knows? You might even become friends now. You would never have guessed this, but your grandpa Frank and I once had a fight."

"No shit!"

"Fuzzy, I thought you were going to start watching your language."

"I mean, no kidding! Is that better?"

"Much better."

Flash asked, "What about the fight you and Grandpa Frank had?"

"It was over a game of marbles. I accused Frank of getting his knuckle on the rim of the circle, and he called me a liar. I gave him a push and he fell over/ That made him mad, so he jumped up and gave me a push. The next thing you know, we were both on the ground punching and kicking and biting."

Fuzzy said, "Wow! You and Grandpa Frank fighting. Who won?"

"I don't think either one of us won. After about five minutes of fighting, we were both out of breath. We both had a bloody nose; we both had skinned-up knuckles, and we were both coughing and slobbering. We had backed away from each other about five feet and were just panting and glaring, when all at once we began to laugh. Frank said, 'All this over a dinky game of marbles.' And we shook hands; we have been best friends ever since."

Flash looked at Fuzzy and asked, "Well, miss prize fighter, do you think you and Margie will ever shake hands and be friends?"

"Huh! Not me and that heifer; she has a face I like to shake hands with."

Grandpa motioned for Fuzzy to come to him. "Sit down here beside me."

She sat down, and he put his arm around her shoulders. "Marvelle, there are always better ways of settling disputes than fighting, and there will always be people like Margie who will call others names. Sometimes I think God must have put people like that on earth just to give others a reason to be tolerant, because as we go through life we will be faced with many challenges that will try out patience. We need to learn how to solve problems with diplomacy instead of war, even if the war is just one on one."

"In other words, Grandpa, you are saying the next time I meet Margie, I should say something like, 'Oh, Margie, how nice you look today; it is so good to see you again. Let's me and you try to be friends.' "

Flash was standing with a big smile across his face, as he was thinking, "Just look at that little wart — hair all messed up and tangled, black eye, torn shirt, skinned-up spots and a swollen-up wrist, and I'm so proud of her I could just bust."

Grandpa hugged her tight and rubbed his chin in her fuzzy hair and said, "I love you, you little monkey."

Ernie's Special Request

SUMMER WAS NEARLY over before going back to school was even mentioned. Then one day Fuzzy phoned Flash, "Did you get a letter from the school today?"

"No, I didn't get no letter. What are you talking about?"

"The teacher sent out letters to all us kids telling us a list of stuff we need to buy before school starts."

"Where do you go to school?"

"Over at Coal Valley. But next year they are going to close Coal Valley and send all us kids to Owappoho. They are building a new grade school there, but it won't be finished until next year, so we get to go one more year to Coal Valley."

"After that, you will going to school where we won that soapbox race."

"Yep. Ain't you going to go to school here this year?"

"Holy karukus, I never thought about going back to school. This has been such a fun summer, I sure never thought about school."

"Hey, Flash, you know how you always fuss at me for cussing?"

"Yeah, it's because you're always cussing."

"What does karukus mean?"

"I don't know. My mom always says it."

"Uh ha, what if it's a cuss word in some other language?"

"Hmm, I don't know."

"Well, let's see. I think I will go out to the toilet and take a karukus."

"You're just trying to be funny."

"No, I ain't; I'm serious. Maybe it means shit in French."

"I guess you could be right. What were we talking about?"

"Do have to you go to school in Topeka?"

"That's where I've been going, but I think I would rather stay here with Grandpa and Grandma and go to school with you and the gang."

"Well, Flash, why in the hell don't you just tell them what you want?"

"You know what? Mom and Dad will be here this weekend, and I think I am going to ask them if I can. But first I'll have to ask Grandma and Grandpa."

"Flash, I've been wondering about something."

"What is it?"

"Well, you have a mom and dad that seem to love you, and all I got is Grandpa Frank. And you have a home in Topeka; yet you live down here with Grandma and Grandpa Tivitts. I can understand why you like to live here. Hell, I'm glad you're here. But now you're even talking about staying down here longer. Are your folks pissed off at you about something?"

"No, Fuzzy, it ain't nothing like that. In fact, the only bad thing about me living here is that I am away from my parents."

"Then how come you have been here all summer, and even want to stay longer?"

"Well, it was like this. My dad had to go to Texas right after school was out last spring, and he had to be down there for a whole month or more. It was some kind of business trip. So, him and Mom let me make the choice between rattling around down there in Texas with them or staying here with Grandma and Grandpa."

"I can see why you didn't want to go on some business trip."

"Yeah. Then when they came back here on their way home, and I was having so much fun with you guys, I asked if I could stay the rest of the summer."

"Then they ain't trying to get rid of you?"

"No, no, no, they ain't trying to get rid of me; they love me."

"Good. But other than you can't bear to think about being away from me, why do you want to stay longer?"

"Because I would like to go to school one year in a small school. And I would like to go to schools with my new friends."

"Oh, and?"

"And, what?"

"Ain't there more?"

"Okay. And, I want to go to school with you. There, I said it."

"I knew it, I knew it, I knew it, I knew it."

That evening at the supper table, Flash mentioned that school would be starting before long. Then he said, "You know something, Grandma and Grandpa? This summer has been the best summer I have ever had. I sure do like staying with you guys, and I sure have a bunch of good friends here."

Grandpa chided, "Oh, yes, Ernie. You do have some good friends here, don't you? Especially that little red-headed Fuzzy."

Grandma spoke up, "Now you quit teasing him about Marvelle. She is just a good friend."

"Actually, Grandma, I really do like Fuzzy a lot. She ain't like most girls. In fact, she is the coolest girl I have ever met. Oh, she cusses a little too much, but she can't help it. Her raising ain't too good. And now she's living with an old bachelor; he probably cusses, too."

Grandpa added, "Yes, Ernie, as you put it, her raising ain't too good. She has had a rough life so far, but she is bright and energetic, and she is tough. She will hold her own in this old world. And old Frank loves her more than anything in this world."

"What I was wondering about is something I need to ask you guys first."

"What is it, Ernie?"

"If Mom and Dad would agree to let me stay here with you guys for this school year, would you let me do it?"

His grandma reached over and took his hand in hers. "Ernie, this has been one of the most enjoyable summers I have ever spent in my entire life. Your grandpa and I would love to have you live with us forever, but we could never be a part in keeping you away from your parents."

"But if they said I could stay here, it would be okay?"

"You know, if Ernie was living with us, they would drive down here a lot more weekends, and we would get to see them more."

"Now, Owen, you sound like you are a part of this plot."

"No, Grandma, Grandpa didn't know a thing about it until right now."

"Your parents are coming down this weekend, so we should be able to settle this question right away."

Ernie could hardly wait until Saturday rolled around. His parents had called and told him they would be in Camp 4 before lunchtime. Grandma was fixing a big dinner for all of them. Flash was even helping his grandmother peel the potatoes and scrape and wash the carrots. It was about 9:30 when the phone rang.

Grandpa answered the phone, then called to Ernie, "Flash, it's for you. It's Fuzzy."

"Hi, Fuzz, what's happening?"

Long pause.

"Can I call you back in a minute?"

"Grandpa, can I invite Fuzzy for dinner? Ain't nobody home at her house but her. Frank is at one of them all-day Lodge meetings."

"I'll call her. You go help your grandma."

Fuzzy answered the phone, "Hi, Flash."

"This isn't Flash. It's Grandpa. What are you doing right now?"

"Nothing."

"Well, Grandma is fixing a big dinner, because Flash's parents are going to be here at noon, and Flash is trying to help her, but he is not very good at it. Could you come over and help Grandma? She really needs you."

"I'll be there quicker than a cat can lick its ass." Click.

Grandpa hung up the phone, sat down on a chair and started laughing.

"What's so funny, Grandpa?"

"Oh, it is just Fuzzy's colorful language."

"What did she say?"

"She said she would be over here quicker than a cat could lick its rear end."

Grandma's voice came from the Kitchen, "And who taught her that? I think I have heard you use that expression more than once, only you don't say rear. You and Frank both encourage that girl because you think it is funny."

"Now, Granny, you know I have come a long way in cleaning up her language. Do you want me to refresh your memory on a few words she does not use any more?"

"No, I don't need to hear them. I guess you and Frank have both helped her. I know you love her and would not encourage her, but just the other day she told me, and I quote, 'Old man Padget is so tight you couldn't drive a flax seed up his butt with a sledge hammer'; only she didn't say 'butt.' Now, where do you suppose she picked that up?"

About that time Fuzzy came bouncing into the kitchen. "What do you want me to do, Granny?"

"Go wash your hands real good, and then come back. I want you to cut up the lettuce and tomatoes for the salad."

"Yeah, I better go wash the crap off my hands first."

"Fuzzy. What three words should you have left out of that last statement?"

She stopped, turned her head up in a thoughtful pose for a moment and then said, "The crap off?"

"Right. Now go wash your hands."

Flash continued to peel potatoes as he was grinning and looking at his Grandpa, who was trying to keep from laughing.

"She really does say some of the same things I have heard you say, Grandpa."

"She does? I guess I am going to have to watch my own language a little closer."

It was 11:30 when Flash's parents' car rolled into the yard, and he ran out to meet them. His mom gave him a long hug and a kiss on the cheek, "Oh, Ernie, it is good to see you. Are you having a good time?"

Ernie's dad gave him a big bear hug and ruffled up his hair. "My golly, Ernie, I think you have grown two inches since we last saw you."

"Mom and Dad, this has been the best summer I have ever had. I have made some great friends. In fact, here is one of them." He gestured toward Fuzzy who was standing on the porch leaning against a post.

"Come here, Fuzzy."

She hesitatingly made her way toward Flash. "Mom and Dad, this is Marvelle Thomas, but we call her Fuzzy. She ain't no relation, but Grandpa claims her as his adopted granddaughter. And we have got to be good friends this summer."

"Hello, Marvelle. Should I call you Fuzzy?"

"Yeah, everybody else does."

"You are several years younger than Ernie, aren't you?"

"No, we're the same age; it's just that I'm a runt."

"She ain't never going to be very big, Mom, 'cause 'big' ain't in her family."

Grandma spoke up, "Marvelle is here today because I needed help in fixing dinner, and she is a good worker. She is going to have dinner with all of us."

Promptly at noon, they all sat down around Grandma's dining room table. Ernie's mom remarked, "Now, Mom, you didn't need to go to all this trouble and fix a fancy meal like this,"

"Fiddlesticks! I don't have a chance to do much cooking like this anymore. I love to do it once in awhile. But I couldn't have done it without the help of Ernie and Marvelle."

"Ernie helped, too?"

Fuzzy spoke up, "He peeled the taters and scraped the carrots, and then him and Grandpa put the extra table leaves in and set up all the chairs. And then he said he would do **all** the dishes."

"Fuzzy! I did not say I would do all the dishes. I said I would help do the dishes."

"I think it would be a big help if he did do them all, don't you, Grandma?"

Ernie's Mom spoke up, "Ernie, I think I will take your place in the kitchen after dinner. You and your dad and Grandpa can go have men talk while Grandma, Fuzzy and I have girlie talk, okay?"

They all sat down around the table. Grandpa said, "Let's all join hands while I ask the blessing."

They joined hands as Grandpa continued, "Dear Lord, thank you for this day, and for this time when family can get together for fellowship and a good home-cooked dinner. Bless this food that it might nourish our bodies, and may our spirits be nourished by the light of your Son Jesus, in whose name we ask these things. Amen."

Fuzzy elbowed Flash and whispered, "You notice he included me in the family?"

With the table cleared and the extra leaves removed, Ernie, his dad and his grandpa went outside to the front porch. Ernie and his dad sat in the porch swing, and Grandpa sat in his wicker chair.

Grandpa said, "Well, son, I guess the old school where you went to grade school is not long for this world."

"What do you mean, Dad?"

"I mean they have consolidated all the schools in this area and are building a new elementary building in Owappaho. Coal Valley will operate one more year."

"You went to school at Coal Valley, Dad?"

"Don't you remember me telling you about the two-teacher school I attended my first eight years. We had one teacher for grades one, two, three and four, and another teacher for grades five, six, seven and eight. Dad, how long did Mr. and Mrs. Cunningham teach at Coal Valley?"

"I think they must have been there at least 25 years. And then when they retired, the board hired another married couple, Al and Amy Timms. I think you went to school with Al."

"Oh, yeah, Al was just one year ahead of me. I had several classes with him, and then we were on the football team and the basketball team in high school. We were good friends."

Ernie was wide-eyed. "I met Mr. Timms the other day, and I really like him. And you really went to school here?"

"Of course, I did, son. This is where I was raised. You knew that; you just forgot."

"I guess I wasn't paying much attention. It really didn't mean anything to me before, but now it does."

"Well, I sure did go to school here. And I think I had as good an education as anybody got in those days."

"You know what, Dad? Your old school is only going to be here one more year, and then they are going to tear it down. And I would like to stay here with Grandma and Grandpa for the rest of this year so I could go to school one year where you went to school."

Ernie's dad was taken aback. "Ernie, you are serious about this, aren't you?"

"Yes, Dad, I am serious. I'll be in the seventh grade this year, and I would like to go to Coal Valley with all my new friends."

"Huh! How about that? You want to go to school where I went when I was a kid."

"Do you think Mom would be in favor?"

"Now, I didn't say I was in favor. Your mom and I will discuss it tonight."

Later that evening, after Ernie's parents, Henry and Alice Tivitts, were settled into bed, his dad said, "Guess what? Ernie wants to stay here with his grandma and grandpa and go to school at Coal Valley."

After a long pause, his mother responded, "Somehow that does not surprise me one little bit."

"It doesn't?"

"No, it doesn't. Did you notice how he looks at that little 'Fuzzy' creature?"

"Fuzzy creature! Oh, for crying out loud, Alice, the kid is only 12 years old."

"Twelve-year-old girls can get pregnant. Or did you know that?"

Henry sat up in bed. "Now, Alice, are you upset because he asked me and didn't ask you?"

"Well, when did he ask you?"

"After dinner, when Dad and I and Ernie went out on the porch, the subject of me attending Coal Valley came up. I mentioned I thought I received as good an education there as I would have anywhere."

"And that is when he asked?"

"Yes. That is when he asked."

"And what did you tell him?"

"I told him I could not answer his question until you and I had talked about it."

"What did your dad think about it?"

"Now you know the folks would love to have Ernie live with them."

(Long pause)

"Henry, I shouldn't have called that little girl 'that Fuzzy creature.' She is a sweet child. A little rough around the edges, but sweet, nonetheless. I didn't mean that. And I can see that she and Ernie are just friends. Heck, it's understandable, seeing how much your folks love the little rascal."

Henry lay back down. "I really don't know what to say about him staying here. It would only be for one year, because the school is closing at the end of the term."

"Coal Valley is closing? Why?"

"They have consolidated with Owappaho, and they are building a new elementary school there."

"I think I remember your mom mentioning that last spring."

"Well, Alice, what do you think?"

"I have to be honest about something. I have always wondered what it would be like to attend one of those little rural schools. I have been a bit envious of many of the tales you have told about your experiences in a multi-graded classroom."

"You have?"

"As much as I would hate to be away from Ernie for a whole school term, I have to admit, it would probably be a wonderful experience for him."

"Then you would agree to allowing him to do it?"

"Do you want him to?"

"I think, if we do allow him to go to school here, there should be a firm understanding it would be for one year only. He would have to agree to come back home, no questions asked, as soon as this school term ends."

"I agree with that. Let's sleep on it. If we still feel the same way in the morning, we will tell him at the breakfast table."

The following morning, Ernie was eager to hear what his parents had decided. He was up and dressed before anyone else in the house was awake. He tiptoed around the morning darkness, being careful to make no noise. He made his way to the kitchen where turned on the light and decided to fix himself something to eat. He was searching through the many leftovers in the refrigerator when the telephone rang.

Hurrying to the phone, he grabbed the receiver and in a low voice said, "Fuzzy, this has got to be you, ain't it?"

"I saw a light in the window, so I figured you would be up."

"What are you doing up so early? It ain't even daylight yet."

"I wanted to know what your folks decided. And talk a little louder. I can't hear you very good."

"I can't talk louder because nobody else is awake and I don't want to wake them up. And you want to know about what?"

"About you going to school here, dummy. What else would I be calling this early for?"

"How did you know about that? I never told you, 'cause I didn't want to say anything until I knew for sure."

"Grandpa told me about it. He said he had a feeling they might let you stay."

"Grandpa told you?"

"Yes, he told me. Me and your grandpa are real good buddies."

"I know you are, Fuzzy. I think he likes you as good as anyone in the whole family."

"Do you know anything yet?"

He whispered, "No, I don't know anything yet. I haven't talked to anybody this morning. I'll let you know as soon as I find out."

"I'm coming over there, Flash."

"No! Fuzzy, don't come over — Fuzzy! Fuzzy!"

Flash mumbled softly to himself as he gently replaced the receiver, "That little turd. Now she is going to be here before anyone else even gets up. What am I ever going to do with her?"

From directly behind him, Flash heard, "Maybe you and her and I should go out in the kitchen and have a talk."

Flash jumped like he was shot. "Mom! I didn't know you were up. You scared the wits out of me."

"I heard the phone ring."

"Was you right there while I was talking to Fuzzy?'

"Yes. I was coming to answer it when you did."

"Could you hear what we were talking about?"

"You really like that little girl, don't you, Ernie?"

"Mom, I have made a lot of great friends this summer, and she is one of them."

"How many of the rest of them are girls?'

"Well, actually there are mainly just six of us in the 'close friend' bunch."

"And how many of that six are girls?"

"Fuzzy is the only one. But, Mom, she ain't like most girls."

Ernie and his mother were seating themselves at the kitchen table when Fuzzy came in the kitchen door.

"Oh, hi, Mrs. Tivitts. I thought Flash was the only one up. Hi, Flash."

"Good morning, Marvelle. My, it's kind of early. Do you always get up this early?"

"No, only if there is something real important coming up."

"Hmm, then there must be something important coming up this morning, right?"

"Oh, you bet there is. What did you guys decide?"

"Decide about what?"

"About Flash going to school this year with me. What else could be so important?"

Ernie's mother dipped her head, covered her mouth and tried to hold back a real laugh, but she could not help chuckling at the frank honesty displayed by this little 'Fuzzy creature.' "

"Come here and sit down with Ernie and me."

With Ernie sitting on one side and Fuzzy sitting on the other, Alice put an arm around the two kids as she said, "Ernie, your dad and I have decided to allow you stay with Grandma and Grandpa …"

She did not get her sentence finished when Fuzzy leaped to her feet and yelled, "YEEEEE-HAAAAAA!" Flash and his mom both stood up. Then Fuzzy threw both arms around Alice and hugged her so tightly she could hardly breathe. She released Alice and went to Ernie and hugged him."

Alice was speechless, and so was Ernie.

Suddenly Fuzzy stopped her celebration and turned to Alice.

"Mrs. Tivitts, I guess you could see that I am tickled over Flash getting to stay here, but I want you to know that Flash and me are just good friends. Oh, I have kissed him a few times, but we ain't having sex. And what's more, we ain't going to start having sex. Hell, we haven't even thought about it. We're both too young for that."

Alice was in complete shock. She stood transfixed a full minute. Then as she glanced at the kitchen door, where she could see her husband and her in-laws standing in their sleeping attire, she said, "Well — ah — that is very … ah … reassuring, Marvelle."

After a long moment, the realization of his mother's answer soaked in to Ernie's consciousness. "Then I do get to stay here for the seventh grade and go to school where Dad went?"

His dad spoke up, "Yes, Ernest, we have decided to allow you to go to Coal Valley this year. However, you must understand, and you must agree, the stay will be for the upcoming year only. You will come back home as soon as school is out."

"I understand, Dad. Thanks."

All of a sudden Ernie was caught up with an emotion he had not experienced. He felt a tightening in his throat and in his jaw muscles, and tears began to well up in his eyes. He stood motionless as his parents both came to him. He could not talk. They had a three-way family hug. Then he went to his grandparents for another three-way hug.

After several moments of everyone fighting back tears, Ernie turned to look at Fuzzy.

She said, "Ain't I going to get a one-way hug?" as she went to him and put both arms around his waist.

"You almost cried, didn't you?"

"Yeah, I guess it is because I'm going to have to put up with you until next June."

Fuzzy punched Flash in the belly as she stepped back. "I ought to snatch you bald-headed, you stinkin' fart."

Everybody laughed as Grandpa put both arms around Flash and Fuzzy.

"This is going to be a great year. Yep. This is going to be a great year."

The Long Shot

THE FIRST TWO months of school at Coal Valley were pretty much routine for Flash as far as academic lessons were concerned. Things were certainly different than he had experienced during his first six years. Probably the most significant thing was the fact that there were only six students in the seventh grade. And they were the same kids with whom he had spent the summer, Fuzzy and her boys.

It was a little difficult getting used to being in one classroom with students in the fifth, sixth, seventh and eighth grades. Even with four grades involved, there were still less than half the number of kids Flash had been accustomed to being with.

Flash really liked his new teacher, Mister Timms. Up until the first of November, the only playground game they played was softball work-up and some touch football, but when November came around, Mr. Timms started them working on a basketball team. There were two boys in the eighth grade who lived on farms located several miles from town, but neither one of them was interested in basketball, so Mr. Timms started working with Flash, Bugs, Foxtail, Knuckles and Squarehead.

What Mr. Timms didn't know was that those five boys had already been practicing quite a bit of basketball out at Mr. Ketterman's barn. He was really surprised when the five boys asked him if they could show him the offense they had been practicing.

Mr. Timms said, "What offense are you boys talking about?"

Fuzzy was listening in the background, and she came forward, "They're talking about the star offense."

Mr. Timms said, "Let me see this so-called star offense."

Fuzzy said, "Okay, guys, I'll be Mr. Ketterman. Bugs, you get the ball and take the top point. Flash, you take the right front point. Foxtail, you take the left front point. Squarehead , you take the right lower point, and Knuckles, you take the lower left point. When I whistle, you start the rotation. (She put her thumb and her middle finger in her mouth and blew a loud whistle.)

Bugs faked a pass to Flash, then made a quick pass to Foxtail. As soon as he released the ball, he made a rolling screen near the point where Flash was stationed. Flash cut around the screen and went to the hoop as Foxtail bounce-passed the ball to him. In the meantime, Knuckles and Squarehead were moving out toward the corners. With the middle now open, Flash hit an easy lay-up.

Mr. Timms said, "Hey, guys, I like that. You say that old man Ketterman taught you guys that play?"

"Yes, he did. He also taught us how to rotate positions in that star formation so that any one of us might be open for a shot. Every time one guy makes a move, someone else will rotate around and fill the point he just left. That way the offense is always spread out and in a position for a rebound. And in case the other team gets the rebound, we are in positions to set up a defense real quick.

Mr. Timms told them, "Well, boys, we don't have a gymnasium and we can't even practice when the weather is bad, but it looks we might be able to have a pretty fair team."

"Who are we going to play?"

"Truthfully, we have only one game scheduled with another school. We are too small to be in a league, but Owappaho has agreed to play us one game on their court. It will be their first game of a 10-game season. Next year all you boys will be going to school there, too."

"Do you think we can beat them, Mr. Timms?"

"They are pretty confident we can't even come close. Their coach said the only reason he was playing us was so he could see all of his boys play before their regular games started."

That made Fuzzy's boys even more determined. They decided to walk out to Ketterman's every day after school and have a practice. Mr. Ketterman worked with the boys until they had that offense down pat.

Now it was time to see if it worked against another team.

When the game started, Knuckles was able to jump high enough to tip the ball out to Bugs. He dribbled down the center of the court, and they set up their five-point star formation. Fuzzy whistled from the sideline, and the movements began. Within 10 seconds, Coal Valley was ahead 2-0.

The game developed into an offensive contest. The Coal Valley boys had concentrated on perfecting that star offense, and they had it down pat. However, their defense was not too good.

Owappaho had a great offense and a pretty good defense, but the Ketterman star offense had too many variations for the Owappaho five to stop. Consequently, the game was nip and tuck right up until the final minute. The lead changed hands 16 times, and the score was tied 15 times.

With 10 seconds remaining in the game, Foxtail hit a hook shot, bringing the score to 62 for Coal Valley and 61 for Owappaho. The Owappaho coach called a time-out. They now had 10 seconds to work the ball in for a shot. And the Coal Valley boys had to be careful not to foul, while at the same time they had to play good defense.

The referee handed the ball to an Owappaho player for the toss-in.

He used four seconds before he managed to find an open player. Then he made a pass to one of his players. That player made a couple dribbles and attempted a bounce pass to their leading scorer under the basket, but the pass was batted away by Flash. Foxtail tried to catch the ball, but it was batted again by an Owappaho player. This time the ball was recovered by Squarehead near the center of the court. He quickly looked up at the scoreboard and saw three seconds remained in the game.

Knowing if he threw the ball high in the air that time would run out before the ball came down, Squarehead grasped the ball in both hands and made a scoop toss of the ball with all his strength. The ball made a high arch that nearly touched the ceiling, but it did not fall where Squarehead intended. The buzzer ending the game sounded when the ball was at its apex of the arch, but it was still in play until it came down.

It came down all right; it nearly ripped the net off the opponents' basket. Coal Valley lost the game 63-62. Fuzzy was the first one to go to Squarehead. "Don't worry about it. You did what I would have done. Who would have thought they had a trained ball?"

In the end, both teams went away happy. A good omen for the consolidation.

Tragedy Strikes Camp 4

GRANDMA TIVITTS HUNG up the telephone receiver, sat down in the nearest chair and brought her apron up to her eyes, "Oh, no! Oh, God, no! Oh, Lord, I have been praying this would not happen."

Grandpa looked up from his paper, "What? What in the world has happened?'

"That was Maude Higgins. She told me that little Fortino girl has polio."

"Oh, my God. Who told her so? Did she say how bad it was?"

"She said it was real bad. They have the child in Kansas City and she is in an iron lung. It has settled in her diaphragm and rib muscles, and they are afraid it is settling in her heart now."

Flash was taking all this in with wide-eyed wonderment. "What is an iron lung, Grandpa?"

"It is sort of a long hollow tube that doctors put people in when they can't breathe for themselves. It does the breathing for them?

"How could something like that breathe for you?"

"I am not sure how they work, Ernie, but a lot of polio victims have to be put in them, at least for awhile."

"Is Brenda going to die?"

"We don't know, son. We hope and pray that she makes it, but if it settles in her heart, it does not look good."

"But her mom is a nurse; she'll know what to do. She knew what to do when Foxtail cut his hand that time."

"I'm afraid this damned polio is something none of us can do anything about. It is some kind of germ that doctors haven't found a cure for."

"I know; other kids can get it, too?"

"Yes, they can. Like I say, the doctors don't know what to do about it right now, but they are all trying to find a way to stop it."

"Ain't Brenda the only one around here to get it?"

"She is the first one we have heard about."

"I wonder if Foxtail knows about it. I'm going over there to talk to him."

Flash ran out the door with his grandma calling after him to stop, but he paid no heed. He ran as fast as his legs could carry him to Foxtail's home. Before he reached their house, he could see Foxtail sitting on the front steps with his head down and his hands up to his face.

He thought, "He already knows about it."

Flash slowed to a walk and continued on until he was standing beside his friend.

"Flash, I just heard that Brenda is very bad sick." He had been crying.

"Yeah, I heard about it, too. She's got polio."

"Yeah, and they said she was real bad with it. She might even die."

"Are you sure? Who told you?"

"Her aunt just called my mom. She said Brenda's dad thought us kids should know."

Flash sat down on the steps beside his friend. There were tears in his eyes.

Within five minutes, Bugs, Squarehead, Knuckles and Fuzzy were all there. This time there was no teasing Foxtail about Brenda. He was most affected by the news, but all of them were very concerned about Brenda.

Squarehead spoke up. "I think we should all huddle up and say a prayer for her."

"You're right," Bugs responded. "You say the prayer, Squarehead. You're the one that's been to cat-kizum and that other stuff."

"Okay. Let's all hold hands in a circle."

They stood by Foxtail's front steps and made the circle.

"Bow your heads, everybody." They bowed their heads, and Squarehead continued, "Lord, I don't know much about praying for somebody who is as sick as Brenda, but we are all her good friends and we are concerned about her. She was on our baseball team, and she likes to be with us anytime she can, and we like to have her, too. Brenda and Foxtail are real good friends. So, Lord, we are praying right now that you will help her get well. That's all we ask right now. Amen."

Foxtail said, "Thanks, Squarehead. I hope God heard us because they said the polio was working on her heart muscle, and that's real bad."

Flash spoke up, "I have heard about polio, but I thought it just made people have crippled arms or legs. But I guess if it can affect leg and arm muscles, it could affect any muscle, and the heart is a muscle."

An hour passed while Fuzzy and the boys sat on the front step of Foxtail's home and talked about the times they had enjoyed with Brenda.

They heard the telephone ring, and a deadly silence settled over the small group. After a minute of two, Foxtail's mother came to the front door. It was painfully obvious she did not have good news. She hesitated for a long moment, and then through a stream of tears, she blurted, "Brenda didn't make it."

Fuzzy went directly to Foxtail. She was crying as she put her arms around Foxtail. "That damned polio. Why in the hell did it have to get Brenda?"

Flash said, "I guess God only knows."

"God only knows! God only knows! Where in the hell was God? If he is a loving God, why in the hell didn't he answer our prayer and do something about this shitting polio?"

"Maybe God can't do anything about it. I think there are lots of things that God can't do anything about," Flash added.

Fuzzy continued, "Well, it's too damn late to do anything about Brenda. Now she's dead and laying on some damned cold slab up there in Kansas City."

Foxtail looked up at Fuzzy. "Fuzzy, I think God is just as sad about this as we are. Flash is right; there are some things He can't do anything about."

"Well, shit on him then. I'm done with him. That's the kind of stuff God is supposed to be good at, and if he ain't no good at it, piss on him."

Flash put his hand on Fuzzy's shoulder. " You shouldn't talk like that. We're all upset right now, Fuzzy. We just ain't used to knowing what to do if somebody we love dies."

All of the kids were in a state of shock. All they could do was huddle close around Foxtail and try to comfort each other.

Two days later, a man from the mortuary in Owappaho came to Camp 4 to talk to the kids about funeral arrangements. Brenda's parents had requested the six kids from Camp 4 serve as pallbearers. They all told the man they knew nothing about what they should do, but they wanted to do it.

On the day of the funeral, a big black car came out to Camp 4, stopped at each of the kid's houses and picked them up. Fuzzy was the last one to be picked up, and all the boys were surprised when she stepped out of the house. None of them had ever seen her wear a dress.

As she stepped into the car, she said, "No remarks about this dress. Grandpa Frank got me this whole outfit, shoes and all, just for today. I'm doing this for Brenda, not for you turkeys."

The car was almost to Owappaho before Flash said, "Fuzzy, you look real nice in that dress, don't she, guys?"

They all agreed.

Bugs added, "Brenda would think you look good, too."

It was a heartbreaking experience for all of them as they unloaded the small white casket containing their friend from the hearse and walked slowly to the gravesite. The funeral was a closed casket affair because of the gut-wrenching fear of polio and the concern that other kids might also get it.

The priest, who was also a family friend of the Fortinos, was so affected by Brenda's death that he had much difficulty in conducting the graveside service. He did not talk more than five minutes.

Flash, Fuzzy, Foxtail, Squarehead, Knuckles and Bugs stood in a line behind the flower-draped casket with tears streaming down their faces as the priest delivered the short eulogy, but the instant the last amen was pronounced, Foxtail ran for the car, and the others all joined him.

Inside the car again, they all sat silent and sobbed. A few minutes passed before Fuzzy remarked, "How do we know she was even in that casket? They never did open it up."

Foxtail answered the question. "She was in it, Fuzzy. I saw her in there last night. My parents took me over to the funeral home. At least her body was in it, but she wasn't there no more."

"What do you mean — her body was in it but she wasn't there?" Bugs asked.

"When I went in that room and seen her laying there, she just looked like she was sleeping. She had on a pretty pink dress and her hair was fixed up real nice; her hands were folded together across her belly, and she was holding some beads with a cross on them. I stood looking at her a little bit; she looked like she would open her eyes and start talking. But then I reached out and put my hand on her hands. She was cold and stiff. Whatever was in her that made her Brenda was gone.

Fuzzy spoke up again in a sobbing outburst, "Oh shit! She was the only girl around here that was my age and size; I was just getting to know her good. Then that son-of-a-bitching polio came along, and God didn't do a damn thing to stop it." She slammed her fist against the back of the front seat.

Squarehead spoke up. "Fuzzy, please quit cussing. And please quit blaming God. He is liable to reach down here and punish you good."

"Just let him try. I'm pissed off at him." She looked upward and said, "Come on, God, punish me for being honest about how I feel. Hit me hard, right here on the chin. I ain't a damn bit afraid of you."

She fell back into the seat and began crying uncontrollably. Flash pulled her up to him and held her shaking little frame close. "It's going to be tough on all of us, Fuzzy. We will never forget her, but we still have each other."

Ernie Goes Home

THE SCHOOL TERM is nearly over, and Ernie has completed all assignments required for him to be passed on into the eighth grade. The teacher, Mr. Timms, has explained to all the Coal Valley students that they would be going to school in the new building in Owappaho next year. He also told them he and Mrs. Timms would be teaching in the new building.

Most of this was passing right over Ernie's head, because he knew he would be going home to Topeka as soon as this school term ended, that he would be coming back to Camp 4 on a few weekends and, perhaps, a week or so vacation during the summer, but he would be going back home to live as soon as school was out. Ernie had agreed to "not even ask" to be allowed to stay. He didn't realize what a bitter pill he would have to swallow. He considered many times about going back on his word and getting down on his knees and begging, but his upbringing would not allow him to backslide.

Without realizing it, Ernie has gotten himself into a situation that is much more emotional than anyone could have imagined. He loves his parents and he has missed them sorely many times over the past year. He realizes he has missed many activities that are available in any school as large as Topeka, but he really does not think this one year at Coal Valley has hampered his learning process. If anything, it has enhanced his education. He is happy with his friends and cannot bear the thought of leaving them.

Ernie is now 13 years old. During the time he has spent in Camp 4, he has grown three inches and gained 25 pounds. He is strong and healthy. Educationally, he well prepared to be advanced to the eighth grade. He is certainly not looking forward to the experience.

The last week of the school term finally arrived. Ernie's days at

Coal Valley are nearly over; his mother and father will be in Camp 4 on Saturday, and he will be going back to Topeka with them on Sunday afternoon. He is sitting at the breakfast table with Grandma and Grandpa. His grandpa remarked, "Well, Ernest Owen 'Flash' Tivitts, this has been quite a year, hasn't it?"

"Yes, Grandpa, this has been quite a year. It has been a fast year, especially the last month."

Grandma spoke up, "It has been a wonderful time for me."

She was saying more, but Ernie could not hear because his emotions were ready to explode. He felt a tightening in his gut, his throat had a lump in it as big as a football, and his eyes were starting to well up. Suddenly, he lost it all and began sobbing with heavy, jerking breaths. He leaned his head down on his folded arms and wept like he had never wept before. Through his shaking sobs, he said, "I can't help it, Grandma and Grandpa. All week I have been about to bust wide open. I'm all tore up in my head."

Grandma and Grandpa were both standing by his side, trying to comfort him. Grandma said, "We understand, Ernie; we understand." She, too, was fighting her emotions.

Ernie continued, "I really like living with you guys, and it was so great to go to school where Dad went, and —"

He didn't finish his remark because his grandpa spoke with a stern, and even gruff, tone Ernie had not heard before.

"Ernie, get hold of yourself! You are not helping the situation by losing control of yourself."

Ernie stopped crying as if a switch had been turned off in his brain.

Grandpa said, "Get up; we're going for a walk."

The two of them walked out of the house and down the road a full half block before another word was uttered. As they left the house, Ernie was wondering, "Why is Grandpa mad at me? I never heard him talk so gruff." Without realizing it, Ernie's mindset had changed dramatically. He was no longer feeling sorry for himself; he was thinking about his grandpa's attitude.

Grandpa stopped and turned, facing Ernie. He extended his arms full length and placed his hands on Ernie's shoulders.

"Look me straight in the eye, son," he said in a stern manner.

Ernie did as he was told.

"Now, let's get something straight. If I recall correctly, you made a promise last August, and you agreed to a condition. Is that not correct?"

"Yes, Grandpa, I know what you're talking about."

"Ernie, I will say only one more thing. Any man who will go back on his word is not worth the dynamite to blow his ass to smithereens — and that goes for a 13-year-old boy, too."

Ernie continued looking into his grandpa's eyes for a short moment, as they stood facing one another. Finally Ernie said a simple, "Thanks, Grandpa."

His grandpa pulled him close and hugged him hard. Releasing Ernie, Grandpa said in a much softer tone, "Now, let's go back to the house and finish breakfast."

Walking back toward the house, Grandpa said, "I hope you didn't think I was too tough on you back there; I needed to make a point."

"You made another point, Grandpa."

"Oh, what was it?"

Ernie answered, "You can't make a point by pussy-footing around. Sometimes you have to get mean."

Grandpa put an arm around Ernie. "You're going to be all right, son; you're going to be all right."

The time had finally arrived. Henry and Alice Tivitts had come to Camp 4 to take their son back home with them. Alice could hardly wait, because she had spent a long and many times, very lonesome, year away from her son.

After his talk with his grandpa, Ernie had resigned himself to the reality of the situation. His feelings about leaving Camp 4 had not changed, but the phrase, "not worth the dynamite to blow his ass to smithereens," had made an indelible impression on his mindset. He was not looking forward to saying goodbye to his friends, but he felt he could handle it.

Grandma Tivitts invited all of Ernie's friends over for a farewell party on Saturday evening. The entire evening, Ernie kept emphasizing that he would be back down on weekends, so they could always remain friends and continue to see each other.

It was nearly eleven o'clock before the guests were all gone, everything had been cleaned up and they were all ready for bed. They said their goodnights and went to their separate rooms. Ernie closed his bedroom door and started to remove his clothes as he heard a slight peck on his window glass. At first, he was not sure, so he stood motionless for a moment. He heard it again. He thought as he went to the window, "It's Fuzzy." He could not keep from feeling a surge of happiness.

He opened the window and she crawled in.

"I just had to come see you again." She went to Flash and they hugged each other.

Fuzzy continued, "I don't know what I'm going to do without you here."

"I'll be back to see you whenever I can."

"You say that now. But I know how these things work. Lot's of stuff can happen between now and — whenever."

Flash didn't know what to say or what to do. Here she was, in his bedroom while his parents and grandparents were in two other rooms in the same house. He knew she should probably leave, but he could not tell her to do it.

After a long pause, Fuzzy said, "Flash, let's keep our clothes on and just lay down on your bed together and talk for awhile."

He could not refuse. So they kicked their shoes off and stretched out on his bed. They lay facing each other, and Flash held her tightly, with her neck cradled in his right arm.

"Oh, Fuzzy, I never dreamed I would ever get to like a girl so much."

She kissed him and said, "You don't like me; you love me. Don't you?"

He squeezed her tightly, "I don't know; maybe I do."

"No maybe about it. You love me and I love you. Say it, you turkey."

"Okay, you little fart; I love you."

"Say it again.'

"I love you, Fuzzy. There, I said it. I love you; I know I do."

Fuzzy got up and turned the light off. Then she came back to Flash.

"Fuzzy, what are we going to do if someone opens my door and looks in here?"

"I don't give a shit if they do. We both got our clothes on, and we ain't doing nothing but just laying here. I want you to hug me and hold me tight for a long time."

Flash took a deep breath and exhaled with a long sigh. "Oh, God, this ain't helping things a bit, but I don't want you to leave." He buried his face into her fuzzy hair.

A long moment passed before she turned her face up and said, "I don't think we should do it, but if you want to have sex, I'll do it."

Flash held her tightly and said, "Oh Fuzzy, Fuzzy, Fuzzy, Fuzzy. You little turd. Of course, I want to have sex with you, but you know, and so do I, that we ain't ready for that yet."

"Good. Then we won't. I was afraid you might say yes, and then I would get knocked up."

They both laughed as Flash was whispering, "Shush, don't giggle so loud."

Ernie was awakened by a knock on his door, followed by Grandpa's voice. "Come on, Ernie, get dressed; breakfast is almost ready."

Fuzzy popped straight up like a cork, "Holy shit, Flash! We went to sleep. It's morning."

Ernie was sitting up and rubbing his eyes when the door opened, and in stepped his grandpa. Grandpa shut the door behind him and put his finger to his lips, indicating for them to be quiet.

Fuzzy said, "We ain't been doing anything wrong, Grandpa. See, we both got our clothes on. We were just talking and we must have fallen asleep."

"Ernie, has she been here all night?"

"Yes, Grandpa. But what she said is true. We were just talking and we fell asleep."

He stood motionless, with his hand to his chin, as he was thinking. Fuzzy and Flash were standing in front of him, wondering what he was going to say.

"Okay, I believe both of you. However, I think we will keep this little 'activity' between the three of us. Fuzzy, does Frank have any idea where you are?"

"He was sound asleep when I left last night, and lots of times I am up and gone somewhere before he gets up."

"Fine. Here is what we are going to do. Fuzzy, you crawl back out that window and wait by the side of the house for a minute or so. I will go back to the kitchen and make sure everyone is in there. I will then say I have invited you to join us for breakfast, that you should be here any minute."

Fuzzy crawled out the window, Ernie went to the bathroom, and

Grandpa joined the rest of the family in the kitchen.

He said, "Where is Fuzzy? I invited her to join us for breakfast."

Grandma added, "My goodness, it is unusual for that little monkey to be late for anything."

About that time, Fuzzy burst into the kitchen and headed straight for the bathroom.

"I'll be back in a minute. I forgot to pee before I left home, and I'm about to bust."

They all laughed, but somehow Grandpa thought it was funnier than the others did.

Ernie's mother said, "My Lord, that child looked like she had slept in that outfit. And for sure, a comb has not touched her hair this morning."

Henry said, "Alice, she lives with an old bachelor."

Grandma added, "Frank loves that child with all his heart, and he tries the best he knows how. Sometimes it appears as if he is not doing a very good job, but believe me, love conquers all."

Grandpa thought to himself, "It starts out pretty early, too."

Fuzzy Was Right

IT WAS THANKSGIVING in 1938 before Ernie got a chance to return to Camp 4. As soon as all family greetings were completed, he picked up the phone and called Fuzzy. He let the phone ring eight times before he gave up and replaced the receiver. He turned from the phone with a look of rejection on his face.

"Grandpa, have you seen Fuzzy lately?"

"Yes, as a matter of fact, I saw her yesterday morning. She and her Grandpa Frank were here for a few minutes. Frank told me a real shocker."

Ernie's dad asked, "What kind of a shocker did Frank have to tell you?"

"I'm not sure you even knew about this, but when Frank was about 40 years old, he almost got married."

"No kidding, Dad? Frank almost got married?"

"Yes, he was dating one of the Owappaho high school teachers, but she backed out on him."

"I think I remember you and Mom talking about that."

"Well, now, here comes the kicker. She wrote Frank a letter a week or two ago. She is still single, and she never really got over Frank. What do you think about that?"

"Well, I'll be damned. She is surely retired by now, isn't she?"

"Yes, she is retired and lives in Joplin. Frank drove over there and took her out for supper last week."

Ernie was listen intently to all this. He said, "Grandpa Frank has a girlfriend? Holy Karukus. What does Fuzzy think about her?"

"Oh, she is all excited about it. She can't wait to meet her. That's where they are today."

"Fuzzy won't be here today?"

"No, they are going to Joplin. Gretchen is fixing a Thanksgiving dinner for them. Her name is Gretchen Krueger. I think they plan to spend the Thanksgiving vacation with her."

Ernie thought, "Fuzzy was right. Lots of things can happen between now and — whenever. I'm not going to see her on this visit."

Indeed, Fuzzy was right. Many things began to happen. Squarehead and his parents moved to Middleton; Bugs has a girlfriend in Owappaho, and they are thicker than molasses in January. With the closing of Coal Valley, Knuckles' parents moved to Owappaho and, Foxtail seems to want to spend as much time as he can with Brenda's mom and dad.

During the Christmas break, Grandma and Grandpa Tivitts came to Topeka. They not only wanted to spend the time there, but they also wanted to look at a house they were thinking about buying.

Ernie got back on track with his schoolmates and his activities. He never forgot his Camp 4 friends, especially Fuzzy. But his life did go on.

Within a year, Frank Thomas and Gretchen Krueger were married. Fuzzy, dressed in a long-tailed formal dress for the first time in her life, other than when she tried on Mrs. Ketterman's wedding dress, was the maid of honor, because Gretchen asked her. She and Gretchen loved each other from the start. As soon as the ceremony was finished, Gretchen hugged Marvelle and told her, "From now on, I am Grandma." Gretchen sold her place in Joplin and moved in with Frank and Fuzzy. Now, Fuzzy finally has a permanent stable influence in her life. She still slips over to her secret hiding place occasionally. That hideout is the only thing she has left that only she and Flash knew about.

Time moves along, and all the kids become involved in more school activities as they become high school students. Then, while they are high school students, World War II comes into the picture. The boys were all faced with the military draft, so within six months of high school graduation in May of 1942, Flash was in the Army, Bugs was a Marine, Foxtail and Squarehead were in the Navy, and Knuckles was in Naval Airforce training. Fuzzy joined the WAACs and was assigned the job of being personal driver for a Major General.

Luckily, when the war was over, they all returned home. Bugs was wounded during the battle of Iwo Jima. The rest of them all saw combat, but were luckier than Bugs. His injuries were not disabling.

Flash came home and took advantage of the G.I. Bill of Rights. He attended Washburn University with the intention of becoming a lawyer, but somehow he decided to opt for a career in business. He accepted a job with Houghton Mifflin Publishing Company and has been with them four years.

Fuzzy was discharged from the Army after serving two three-year hitches with the WAACs. She came back home to live with Frank and Gretchen while she attended college in Pittsburg, Kansas. She graduated in less than three years with a master's degree and certification in counseling. She also has a contract to be employed by the Dependence, Kansas school system. She earned her B.S. while in the Army.

The Reunion of Fuzzy and Flash

ERNEST OWEN TIVITTS graduated from college four years ago, and at age 28 is successfully employed by a school textbook publisher. Right now he is on a two-week vacation. He is driving south out of Kansas City, Kansas, and he is headed toward that little coal mining settlement in southeast Kansas called Camp 4. He wants to see if the house his grandparents lived in is still there. They moved to Topeka not long after he had spent a year in Camp 4 with them, so he never again had cause to return. He also wants to see if the house where Fuzzy lived is still there, and he might even take a stroll to a certain spot in a pasture where there used to be a large sink hole. But most of all, for some driving reason, he has a real need, if possible, to find out what ever happened to Fuzzy.

As he drives down the old Camp 4 road in the direction of his destination, he can see the house in which his grandparents once lived is standing, but vacant and extremely run down. The front porch is in terrible repair; the yard is full of small trees and large weeds. Ernie stops his car in the driveway, gets out and walks through the weeds to the front door. The door is unlocked, just like it was when his grandparents lived there. He walks through the house and looks into each of the three bedrooms and the kitchen. When he steps into the room in which he slept, there is a sudden scurry of a small animal as it runs and jumps out the slightly raised window.

He looks at that slightly open window, and in his mind, he can see Fuzzy as she was the last time he saw her. He said aloud, "Oh, Fuzzy. How I wish you were there right now."

He looks around his former room and notices the loose wallpaper hanging from the ceiling. A patch of plaster has fallen from the wall and the floors are bare, but the memories are still here. He walks slowly around in every room as the memories bounce around in his head. There is still an old ragged upholstered chair in a corner of the living room. He walks over to it and sits down. He closes his eyes, leans back and relaxes. Before he realizes it, he has drifted off into dreamland. He is a kid again, and he is visiting his grandparents.

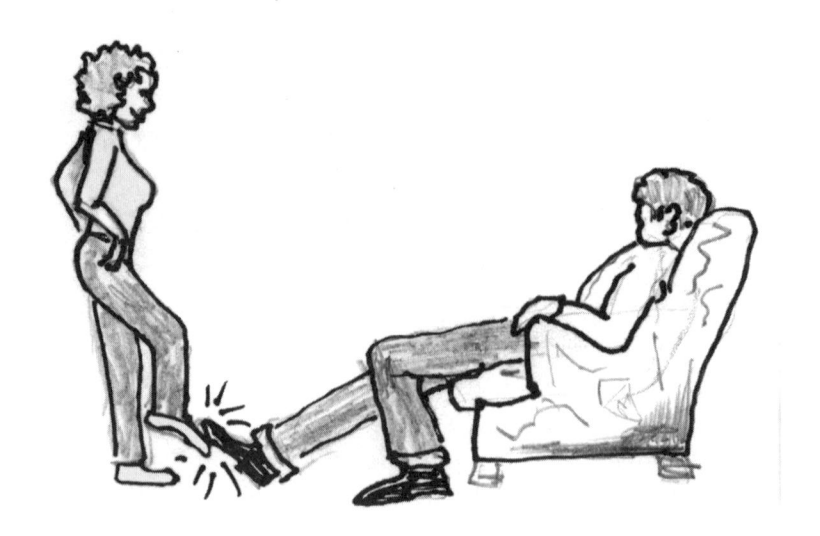

Suddenly Ernie realizes someone is kicking his foot and saying, "Hey, Flash. Wake up; come on Flash, wake up; we have things to do."

As he finally arouses from that deep sleep, he looks up to see a young woman standing in front of him. She is wearing a pair of jeans, a white blouse and tennis shoes. Her hair is dark red and very curly; her eyes are a deep brown and she is smiling from ear to ear. She is a fully mature young woman, but she still has that same look he remembers so clearly.

Ernie jumps to his feet, looks down on her small frame for a moment and says, "Oh, my God! Fuzzy, it is you! It really is you."

She looks up into his eyes and says, "Yes, it is me. When I saw a car parked in this drive, I had to walk over to investigate. You might have grown eight inches and gained a hundred pounds, but I knew it was you the instant I saw you sleeping in that old chair.

Ernie reaches out and gathers her into his arms. He picks her up off the floor and swings her around. He squeezes her so tightly she gasps, "Let me breathe."

He puts her down and holds her at arm's length as he looks her over. She steps back, puts one arm above her head and one hand on a hip as she slowly makes a 360-degree turn. "What do you think of me now?"

"Oh, Fuzzy, you look exactly as I had envisioned you to look."

She answers, "I am a whopping five feet and one inch tall, I weigh 103 pounds, and I am all woman."

They both laugh as she says, "Now let me get a good look at you."

Ernie repeats Fuzzy's moves, as he raises one hand and arm high above his head and places the other hand on his hip. He slowly turns around."

"See, I am quite a hunk now. I am a flat six feet tall and I am 203 pounds of solid muscle."

She reaches out and tries to "pinch an inch" from Ernie's midsection, as he jumps back laughing.

Then he takes her small face into his two big hands, looks deep into her eyes and says, "I have never stopped thinking about you. I never dreamed I would see you again, but I never gave up hope. Oh, Lord, I never quit hoping I would find you again. I just can't believe it is really happening." He hugs her close and looks up as he closes his eyes. "Lord, please don't let this be a dream."

"It is not a dream. I am really here, and you are really here. I, too, never dreamed this would actually happen, but I never quit hoping this day would arrive. Now kiss me, you big turkey."

"Now let's go over to Grandpa Frank's. I want you to meet Grandma Gretchen."

"Oh, yeah, I remember that he married his old girlfriend. Are you living with them now?"

"No, I live in Dependence, but I try to get over here at least once or twice a month to check on them. Grandpa is now 84, and Grandma Gretch is 81. But they are both healthy."

"What do you do in Dependence?"

"I am a school counselor."

"The heck you are?"

"Does that surprise you?"

"Fuzzy, nothing you ever did, or ever will do, will really surprise me."

"Tell me you're not married, Flash."

"No, Fuzzy, I have never even had a steady girlfriend."

"Oh, poof, a big handsome guy like you; get out of here."

Ernie stops walking and turns Fuzzy facing him. "Fuzzy, I never forgot that last night I lived with Grandma and Grandpa. We were only 13 years old, but as we lay on my bed in the dark that night, fully dressed, and I told you I loved you, I meant it. I will never go back on those words. I never stopped loving you."

"Flash, I knew I loved you a long time before that night. I guess we are hooked on each other."

Ernie asks, "What do you think we should do about it?"

"That's up to you, you big turkey."

"Why don't we just run off and get married?"

Fuzzy jumps off the ground, throws her arms around Flash's neck and her legs around his waist. "I was afraid you were never going to say that. But my answer is, you damn right I will. The sooner the better."

When Ernie finally put her down, he said, "That is the first cuss word you have uttered today. What happened?"

"You sure have put on the weight, Fuzzy!"

"You're just getting weak, you big TURKEY!"

She laughs. "Oh, I still know all of them, probably a few more. But when I made a decision to work with young girls, I decided to give up cussing. Unless, of course, I get cut off in traffic, or somebody tries to shit on me."

Ernie laughs. "We are going to have a lot of interesting tales to tell our kids, aren't we?"

"Yes, we are, and I can hardly wait to get started."

"Having kids or telling stories?"

She looks up at Ernie and says with a mischievous twinkle in her eyes, "Both."

Two weeks later, Mr. Ernest Owen Tivitts and his bride, Mrs. Marvelle Ann Thomas Tivitts, are moving into their recently rented house in Dependence, Kansas. She will continue her job as girls counselor with the school system, and Ernie will continue his job with the publishing company, only in a different territory; he now works in southeast Kansas.

Old Man Padget's Watermelon Patch

LISTED IN THE obituary section of yesterday's newspaper that lies on the car seat next to Ernie is the name of Ellory Dean Padget, 103 years old. The obit indicates there will be no formal funeral, only a graveside service at 2 p.m. today. Ernie is headed that way because this old man holds a special place in his childhood memory.

The time is 1:35 as Ernie pulls his car to a stop on the road adjacent to a small country cemetery. He steps out of his car and starts walking toward a mound of freshly dug soil that indicates a gravesite. He notices two men who are obviously members of the cemetery work crew, and one man dressed in a business suit.

Ernie walks up to the three men and says, "I assume this is the location of Mr. Padget's graveside service."

One of the men in work clothing answers, "Yes, this is the place. Are you a relative."

"No, I am not a relative, but I knew Mr. Padget about 40 years ago, when I was a boy."

One of the crew members asked, "What is your name?"

"Ernest Tivitts, but in those days I was known as Flash."

When Ernie said Flash, the guy in the business suit said, "Well, I'll just be damned." He extended his right hand and said, "Lawrence Ferguson, better known as Bugs."

As Bugs and Flash were exchanging greetings, two well-dressed men approached. Flash and Bugs both recognized the approaching men. Bugs said, "How about this? Do you recognize these two, Flash?"

Flash answered, "You bet I do. Nearly 40 years might have elapsed, hair is getting gray and middle sections are expanding, but facial expressions do not change; it's Foxtail and Knuckles."

Bugs added, "You're in for a surprise."

The four men were having a great reunion when the funeral home vehicles drove into the cemetery. There were only two vehicles in the procession as it stopped next to the gravesite. The passenger side door on the first vehicle opened, and a priest stepped out. In one voice, three of the four men all said, "Well, I'll just be damned. Squarehead is a priest." Bugs already knew.

Father Oplotski recognized the four men instantly. He said, "I don't think Mr. Padget would mind if we take a few moments for a reunion. They were hugging and shaking hands when the funeral director asked, "Would you four gentlemen like to assist in moving the body to the graveside?"

While Father James Oplotski delivered the short eulogy, Ernie's mind was wandering back to a certain watermelon patch.

It was a warm early fall day as Flash looked up and saw Bugs and Foxtail headed toward the house. He hollered, "Hey, you guys, where you headed?"

Bugs answered, "Hi, Flash, let's go swimming."

"Good idea. I better go tell my grandma where I'm going."

Foxtail added, " We're going by Squarehead's grandpa's on the way. He'll want to go, too."

So the three 12-year-old boys, wearing their usual attire of bib overalls — period, went walking down the dusty road with the hot dust squeezing up between their bare toes, headed for their favorite swimming hole out at the razor pit.

They didn't take the usual route because they knew Squarehead was staying with his grandpa while his folks went somewhere. But they didn't think it was right to go swimming and not tell Squarehead. Bugs had already gone by Knuckles' house and told him; he was supposed to meet them at the railroad tracks.

As they walked down the road, they came upon a big bullsnake that had been run over by a car. Knuckles got his pocket knife out and said, "I'm gonna preform a ortopsy."

So he split open the belly of that big snake and pulled its guts out while the other boys stood and watched. They were all surprised to see that snake had guts and stuff that looked a lot like a squirrel or a rabbit.

When they arrived at Squarehead's, they found he was looking for something to do, so he was raring to go. Squarehead's grandpa had a big pear tree in his yard, so they all took a couple of pears when they left.

Squarehead said, "Hey, guys, let's take a shortcut through Old Man Padget's cornfield. I heard that he plants watermelon seeds out in the middle of the field. They ought to be ripe for the picking about now."

"Good idea," the rest of them all said at once.

So, with Squarehead leading the way, they headed out.

While they were walking down the road, Foxtail noticed Knuckles was slicing his pear with the same knife he just done that autopsy with. He said, "Yuck! Knuckles, ain't that the same knife you used to carve up that dead snake?"

"Shore it is, but I done like this," and he wiped the blade back and forth on his pant leg.

Old Man Padget's farm was directly between Squarehead's grandpa's house and the razor pit. His cornfield was almost ready for shocking, so it was a pretty good guess that the melons would be ready, too; that is, if they could just find the patch out there in the middle of the cornfield. The corn was about as tall as they had ever seen. And it was thick and was a real good stand.

When they got out in what they thought was about the middle, they split up and started looking for melons. It didn't take long before Foxtail hollered, "Here they are, over here."

The four other boys all went to Foxtail, and sure enough, there the melons were. They were those long striped ones. Knuckles started to split one open with his pocket knife, but Bugs picked it up and busted it over his knee, saying, "Oh, no, you don't, not with that knife," and they all started digging in with their hands. All they ate was the heart. They only busted up what they could eat, and then they started toward the swimming hole.

As the boys were leaving, they noticed Knuckles had decided to take one melon with him. He slid a melon in the front of his bib overalls, and they all started teasing him, telling him he looked like a real skinny, knocked-up woman. They were laughing at him as he waddled along with that melon in his bib. Then all at once the melon shifted and slid down his overall leg. It jammed in tight, and they really started laughing.

It was quite a hoot. Knuckles began trying to get that melon out of his overall leg. He was dancing around until he fell over. There was a rock right where he fell, and the melon busted inside his overalls. Even Knuckles was laughing at that.

It was hilarious because Knuckles was having to take his overalls off before he could get that busted melon out of his britches, and he wasn't wearing any shorts, so there he stood, buck naked and dripping with watermelon juice, while the rest of the boys were waiting for him to get his wet overalls back on.

In the meantime, Bugs was inspecting a strange-looking weed. He said, "Look at the size of this weed. And there is another one."

They started looking around and discovered a big patch of these strange-looking weeds a few rows over.

Flash said, "What kind of weeds are they?"

Foxtail looked at them and said, "I don't know, I never seen any that looked like these."

Bugs said, "Why, these weeds are as tall as the corn, and they look a little like a Christmas tree."

Flash said, "I know they ain't ragweeds, and they ain't velvet leaf."

Foxtail was looking at the leaves. "Look here, guys, these leaves all have five little leaves that have saw-tooth edges."

About that time, Squarehead said, "Whoa, guys, you know what I think these weeds are?"

"No, what are they?"

"I think they're that crazy weed. Oh, you know, we studied about them in science class. Remember? Mr. Timms took a whole class period to tell us about how people smoked them and got sort of drunk, and done dumb stuff."

Flash added, "Yeah, that leaf looks like the one in the science book. It's called Mary Warner."

"Bugs added, "No, it ain't Mary Warner, that's what some of us guys was calling it; it's marywanna, that's what it is."

The boys just stood there a looking at each other wide-eyed. Finally, Bugs spoke up. "Now we all know that Old Man Padget is a stingy old fart, but he ain't no crook. I bet he don't know nothing about these marywanner weeds a-growing in his cornfield.

Flash remarked, "Reckon we better go tell him what we found?"

"Maybe we should go tell the marshal."

"Hell, no, we can't do that. He might arrest us for stealing watermelons."

"I think we better jest get out of here and keep our mouths shut."

"Yeah, but what if these weeds don't belong to Mr. Padget and he gets in trouble for growing them on his place?"

Flash spoke up, "I know what to do. We'll tell my grandpa. He knows Mr. Padget; they will figure out what to do. Grandpa says old Padget is a good ole boy, but he is so tight you couldn't drive a flax seed up his butt with a sledgehammer."

Foxtail asked, "What's a flax seed?"

Bugs said, "What difference does it make? We're talking about marywanner now."

Before they realized there was anyone else within a mile of where they were, three strange men snuck up on them from three sides. They were surrounded. One of the men spoke up in a real gruff voice. "What the hell are you little bastards doing out here in this cornfield?"

It scared Flash so bad he almost peed his overalls, and he probably was not alone.

Bugs was the calmest of all of them. He just looked up at that big guy and said, "Well, if you don't tell Mr. Padget about us stealing his watermelons, we won't tell him you guys was here either."

The three guys looked at each other for a moment. Then one of them said, "Have you guys already found the melons?"

Flash answered, "Yeah, we ate our bellies full, and now we are headed for the razor pit for a swim."

One of the men asked, "Where are the melons?"

"Right back there a few rows." Bugs pointed in the direction of the melon patch.

Then one of the men asked, "Do any of you boys know what kind of weed this is?"

They all looked toward the marywanner plants. Then Knuckles said, "I think they must be them giant ragweeds.

Flash added, "Maybe they are what some folks call horse weeds. I guess because they are tall as a horse."

Foxtail took a branch from one of the marywanner plants in his hand and said, "I ain't seen nothing like this before; of course, I ain't much wise on any kind of weed."

Knuckles remarked, "If my Grandma Pointer was here, she could tell us. She's a expert on greens. If these things are fit for eating, she would know about it."

One of the three men sort of chuckled a bit. "I'll bet Old Man Padget is going be pissed off at whoever he hired to cultivate this field for missing this big patch of weeds." They all laughed.

Then one of them said, "You boys better go on about your business. And remember our deal — you don't mention seeing us here stealing watermelons and we don't tell anyone you were here either."

The boys tucked their tails between their legs and got out of there as soon as they could. They forgot all about swimming. But as they were starting back to town, they saw this truck with high sides and a canvas tarp over it parked around the curve under a big tree next to the cornfield.

Bugs says, "Look, guys. I bet those guys come here in that truck."

"Hey, they ain't no doubt about it."

Bugs was the leader of their little gang, so he called everybody into a football huddle and said, "Now, guys, I tell you what we're going do. Knuckles, you and Foxtail go back to town and get the marshal. Tell him what we seen. In the meantime, me and Knuckles and Flash will sneak over closer to that truck an keep an eye on it. Okay, move out."

Two boys took off for town while the other three went closer to the truck. As they approached a spot about 30 yards from the truck, the three men came out of the cornfield; each one of them was dragging three or four of those big weeds. They had cut them off just above the ground. They rolled back the tarp and started loading the weeds into the truck.

"Shhh," Bugs put his finger to his lips. "We have to get close enough to get the numbers off that tag."

Flash said, "I think we're going have plenty of time. That is a big patch for them to cut down and load up." They remained hid behind the tall grass and weeds for what seemed like hours, but next thing they knew, there were two sheriff cars coming slowly down the road and stopping a distance in front of the truck and two more pulling up about the same distance behind it. They stayed back and deputies started pouring out of all four cars. The boys just hunkered down behind the weeds where they were hiding.

About the time all the deputies were in place, the three men came dragging out another batch of weeds and started to load them in the truck.

All at once they hear a whistle, and nine uniformed police officers stand up from their hiding places; they all had guns pointing at the crooks.

One of the crooks slammed his weeds down on the ground and raised his hands in the air. "Those little rotten bastards! We should have knocked them in the head while we had a chance."

That's when Flash and Bugs stood up. The sheriff said, "Good work, boys, that's the best undercover work we have had in this county for years."

Two days later the town had a potluck dinner for the boys. The sheriff was there, and he made a fancy speech about what a great job they done. Then he made each one of them a Special Deputy Sheriff and pinned a badge on them. Everybody clapped real hard, and they just stood there wondering why they should get all that attention.

Then Mr. Padget stood up and said, "I shore am proud all you boys caught them crooks that was using my cornfield to raise their dope." He continued, "And there is something else, boys. There is a watermelon patch out in the middle of that cornfield, and I want you boys to know that you are welcome to go out there and eat all the melons you can hold, anytime you want to."

The boys looked at each other for a bit. Finally Bugs said, "You guys think we should tell the truth?" They nodded their approval.

Bugs went on, "Actually, Mr. Padget, the only reason we happened to find that patch of dope and turn them crooks in was that we was already out there a helping ourselves to your melons."

Mr. Padget answered, "Yes, Bugs, I knew you were there. I also know that none of you boys are bad. It really makes me feel good to hear you admit you were stealing watermelons. And since you boys caught the crooks, I won't charge you for the melons."

Everybody stood up and clapped their hands again. They had turned their stealing into an event that gave them something to really be proud of.

The service ended, but Ernie's mind was still wandering when he

Padget Funeral

felt a hand on his shoulder. Bugs was saying, "It is really good to see you again, Flash. However, we would much rather have seen Fuzzy." He gave Flash a friendly push.

"Our daughter is playing on a volleyball team that is in a tournament today. We try to attend every game in which she plays. Fuzzy didn't know Mr. Padget like we did, so she opted for the volleyball game, but she will be kicking herself when she learns all you guys were here today."

Bugs said, "I guess she didn't know Mr. Padget because she refused to go skinny-dipping with us." They all laughed.

"Do you still call her Fuzzy?"

"Yeah, sometimes I do, when we are by ourselves. But since she is a school counselor now, I try not to call her Fuzzy in the presence of kids."

"Does she still cuss like a pirate?"

Ernie laughed. "No. She said she had to give it up, and I quote, 'Unless someone cuts me off in traffic or tries to shit on me.'"

They all got a belly laugh out of that.

"You tell her we will try to forgive her, but it will be hard," Foxtail added.

Squarehead suggested they all exchange addresses so they could keep in touch.

Knuckles added, "Not only that, we need to have a reunion."

They laughed, they hugged and they exchanged family information. Bugs is the champ in the kid department, with seven. Knuckles is now a grandfather and, of course, Squarehead, is a priest. Foxtail never married. As he shook Flash's hand when they were parting, he said, "Flash, you are so fortunate you have Fuzzy." Tears filled his eyes. "I know Turnip and I would also have made a great team."

Flash could not say a word. He put both arms around Foxtail and embraced him warmly.

Suddenly, Bugs said, "Hold on a minute, guys. We have some important business before the house, and we need to take a vote." They all stopped and looked in Bug's direction.

He continued, "Knuckles mentioned in passing that we needed to have a reunion. He is right. Not only do we need one, we are going to have one."

They all nodded in agreement. Flash said, "What do you have in mind, Bugs?"

He went on to say, "I am in the fireworks business. I have 10 of those big fireworks tents that I loan out to various organizations every July. Along with the help of my family, I always set up and run the one in Owappaho. Come next July, I would like to leave that tent up after the fireworks are all removed and host a Camp 4 reunion in it. What do you think?"

Father Squarehead said, "Great idea, Bugs. I'll help you get it organized."

Flash was delighted. "Oh, I know Fuzzy would vote for this idea; I'll vote for her."

Bugs continued, "All those in favor, let it be known by the usual sign of gang vote." The vote was unanimous.

Squarehead said, "I'll get together with Bugs, and we will work out the details. I have all your addresses and phone numbers. I will handle the secretarial chores, if that is okay with everybody?"

They all left with a light heart, knowing what could be in store next July.

The Annual Camp 4 Picnic

BUGS AND SQUAREHEAD have done an excellent job in organizing the first annual Camp 4 Picnic. Bugs has made arrangements to have the all meals catered by Chicken Annie's and the entertainment provided by members of a local polka band, featuring Jarbo Watson on banjo and guitar, Johnny Zibert on accordion.

Since Bugs and Squarehead were given the total responsibility of organizing the event, they have taken the liberty of setting a permanent date; the Camp 4 Picnic will be held annually on the second Saturday of July. The initial meeting during the current year 1974. Registration will be at 10 a.m., lunch at the help-yourself table, meeting at 1 p.m.; dinner will be at 6 p.m. Entertainment will begin at 7:30 p.m. No set ending time.

In the event of inclement weather, the picnic will be held in Father Oplotnic's Parish Hall.

On the day of the first picnic, people began to arrive at the tent before Squarehead and his altar boys had the registration table set up. He was directing the boys where to place the table when he looked up to see a big guy and a small woman standing a few feet in front of him.

The red-headed woman came to him with her arms extended, saying, "Squarehead, somehow I was not a damn bit surprised when Flash told me you were a priest."

Within a half hour, the tent was buzzing with laughter. Bugs got Fuzzy's attention and asked her, "Fuzzy, if you can still do that loud whistle, I need everybody's attention."

She placed her thumb and her middle finger between her lips, took a deep breath and emitted a whistle with a loudness that even surprised her. "Okay, you turkeys, knock it off. Bugs has an announcement."

When the laughter subsided, Bugs said, "I am thrilled you are all here so early, but we have not had time to set up everything. Just make sure you get registered and pick up your name tag. I know we won't have difficulty recognizing each other, but there are wives, other family members and kids here, too."

Promptly at one o'clock, Bugs asked everyone to have a seat. "The first thing we will do is have introductions. Would each you stand, introduce yourself and then have your family members and guests stand as you introduce them. We'll start with you, Fuzzy."

Fuzzy introduced Frank and Gretchen Thomas, "My grandma and grandpa." Then she introduced 19-year-old Ernest Owen Tivitts, Jr., "Better known as Butch, and 17-year-old Elsie Mae Tivitts, "Better known as Little Britches. Elsie took a playful swing at her mom. Fuzzy continued, "This big lug is Flash, better known as my old man."

Flash stood up and introduced his grandparents. "Of course, this old pair needs no introduction." Owen and Elsie were sitting where everyone could see them, so they just smiled and waved, "I doubt that we could measure the positive influence they have had on all of us.'

Foxtail stood to introduce his guests, Sara and Sam Fortino. Sam asked to have the floor for a moment. "I am almost lost for words. What a wonderful bunch of people you are! You will never know what it meant for Sara and me when that bunch of rag-a-muffin kids took our little girl into their group, all those years ago. We have lost a daughter, but we gained a son." He put his arm around Foxtail. Sara stood, and they had a three-way hug.

Father James stepped forward. "If there is a telescope in heaven, and I am sure there must be, Brenda is certainly looking down on us right now." He paused a moment before he asked, "Okay, who is next? How about you, Knuckles?"

Knuckles introduced his wife, Beulah, and their children. "This is our youngest, eight-year-old Glenn; this is 11-year-old Charles Palmer; this is our oldest boy, Jack; he is 17. And here is our daughter, Kelly, and her husband, Larry Stark. Beulah is holding our granddaughter, six-month-old Emily."

Squarehead's mother, Gertrude Oplotski, was beaming when he introduced her. Then he said, "And now it is Bugs' turn. It is going to take him awhile."

Bugs stood for a short moment before he spoke. "It has really been great to get everybody together again. Of course, Squarehead and I see each other so often we get tired of looking at each other. No, we don't; you know I'm kidding. I have to watch my language around him because he is not only my best friend, he is my priest." He motioned for his wife to come to his side. "Squarehead introduced me to this girl over 20 years ago. This is my wife, Phyllis." Then he mo-

THE FERGUSON KIDS

FUZZY
KNUCKLES
FLASH
TURNIP
SQUAREHEAD
FOXTAIL
BUGS

tioned for their children to come forward. He said, "I have instructed our kids not to wear a name tag, for a reason you will soon know," He lined them up according to age. "Their ages are: 19, 17, 15, 13, 11, 9 and 7." He continued, "Now the surprise: Their names are: Marvelle, Augustus, Ernest, Brenda, Merle, James and Lawrence, Jr."

The Gang members were all surprised and pleased with the names of the Ferguson kids. Then Phyllis stepped forward and announced, "Their nicknames are: Fuzzy, Knuckles, Flash, Turnip, Foxtail, Squarehead and Bugs. How does that grab you?"

The picnic ended with a tremendous round of laughter and applause.

About the Author

CARL A. OTTO was born February 12, 1926, in Pierce, Nebraska. He was the second child in a family of six. From the time he was a toddler, he was a curious, venturesome individual with an inborn drive for excitement, along with an air of confidence that he could do anything. He was not a mean child, but he was an ornery and mischievous one. He was not a good student as a child; however, in spite of not learning to read until third grade, missing all but the first six weeks of the seventh grade and dropping out of high school with a total of nine and one-half credits, he went on to college and earned B.S. and M.S. degrees. His choice of a working career was that of a teacher, athletic coach, high school and elementary school principal, and his last 15 professional years were served as a superintendent of schools.

Although Otto's main source of income during his working days was that of an educator, his summers, weekends and many evenings were spent doing work as a painter, carpenter, plumber, electrician, sports referee, farm hand, cattleman, artist, sign painter, bulldozer operator, wallpaper hanger and even a short stint as a roustabout on an oil rig.

Throughout his lifetime, he has done volunteer work as a scoutmaster, little league coach and umpire, special deputy sheriff, and as a member of civic organizations. He is currently volunteering as a Red Coat hospital worker.

He entered the United States Army in February of 1944 and served 29 months, with two years of duty in Europe. He was an active soldier during three major military campaigns in Belgium and Germany during World War II. He was honorably discharged with the rank of Technician Fifth Grade in the spring of 1946 and remained in the Army Reserves for another three years.

He married Aletha Faye McCants on July 20, 1947, and they were married nearly 54 years when she passed away on April 6, 2001. They had two sons: William Clyde, who is a retired educator now serving as a Kansas state representative, and Kenneth Porter, who is an elementary school principal.

Otto's early childhood was lived in an almost nomadic existence. By the time he entered the military service, he had lived in five different states, 10 different towns and 21 different houses. He is currently living alone in the old farmhouse near Cherokee, Kansas, where his late wife was born and raised.

To order additional books or for more information, contact:

Carl A. Otto
1053 S. 130 St.
Cherokee, Kansas 66724

Phone: 620-457-8606
Cell: 620-724-2084
E-mail: fatkrout@hotmail.com

Price of book = $19.95 retail,
but only $15.00 each if purchased
directly from the author!